SURPRISE ATTACK!

Liz stomped on the man's instep with her heel and then grabbed his hair. She was about to smash his head into the wagon – *that* would wake up the women inside for sure – when moonlight fell on his face and she got a glimpse of a grinning mouth.

John Cody, the Pinkerton man.

"Why you –" she began.

"Scared you, didn't I?"

"Damn right you did!"

He put a finger to his lips, shushing her.

"What did you think you were doing?"

"Taking you away."

"For what?"

"What do you think?"

"You've got your nerve."

"I've got my lust."

"You –"

He stepped close to her and kissed her roughly.

"I want you, Liz."

It had been weeks since she'd been with a man, and her lips tingled from the kiss.

She didn't resist when he took her hand and led her away from the wagon, away from the camp. When they were far enough away, he slid his arms around her and pulled her close. He kissed her again and she kissed back, her mouth open, her tongue searching. She felt him open her shirt and slide a hand inside and caught her breath as his palm brushed her nipples.

ANGEL EYES

ANGEL EYES

#7

SIX-GUN ANGEL

Also by Robert J. Randisi

Angel Eyes

Tracker

Mountain Jack Pike

ANGEL EYES

#7

SIX-GUN ANGEL

Robert J. Randisi

SPEAKING VOLUMES, LLC
NAPLES, FLORIDA
2013

ANGEL EYES
#7 SIX-GUN ANGEL

ISBN 978-1-61232-589-7

To my two little angels, Christopher and Matthew.

CHAPTER ONE

It happened very quickly, and why they picked on her was a question Liz Archer had no time to ask herself. She had just crossed from Utah into Nevada and was looking forward to camping for the night when a bullet whizzed by her ear just seconds before she heard the report of the shot.

She turned in the saddle and saw five or six riders bearing down on her from a distance. Whether they were trail robbers or some misinformed posse — or perhaps they really knew who she was — their mistake had been firing before they'd gotten close enough. Liz felt that she and Blossom would have absolutely no trouble outdistancing the men, thereby avoiding a confrontation that would end with someone's death — possibly even hers.

She urged Blossom into a full gallop, and the powerful horse had not gone a hundred yards when fate intervened, manifesting itself in the form of a chuckhole. The horse's front right hoof went into the hole and she fell, pitching Liz from the saddle. Only the fact that they had not yet been able to attain top speed saved both of them from more serious injury, but the injuries sustained were serious enough.

Blossom went down to her knees, kept herself from falling, and regained her balance, but was unable to put her full weight on her front leg.

Liz flew from the saddle and landed with a thud that knocked her senseless, though not fully un-conscious.

She was aware of the men reaching her, laughing, pawing her, going through her pockets, undoubtedly going through her saddlebags, and finally she was unable to keep herself from falling down a black hole, from which she had no way of knowing if she would ever escape.

When she woke it was dark.

She sat up and took a moment to recall where she was and how she came to be there. Buttoning her shirt, which had been opened to her waist, she heard Blossom nearby and immediately became fearful of the horse's safety. She got to her feet painfully, found the bay mare, and proceeded to examine her. From what she could see, the horse was not seriously injured, but only a vet would be able to tell the full extent of the injury. One thing she did know. There was no way she was going to walk tonight.

"All right, girl it looks like we make camp right here," she said, stroking the animal's neck.

She went through her saddlebags and found that

the thieves had left her little to make camp with. They had taken all of her food, her extra gun — her father's old Walker Colt — and all of her money. For some reason they'd left her holstered Colt Paterson, probably because it was too small a gun for a man to carry. She noticed with regret that her flat, metal ace of spades, given to her by Chance Taker, was also missing.

She scraped up what she could from the area to make a fire and sat warming herself near it. At least they had left her a blanket, although they had taken her bedroll. She had found some beef jerky at the bottom of one saddlebag and chewed on it while reviewing the incident in her mind.

She now knew that it had been a simple robbery, although she could still feel the hands of her pursuers on her while she lay semiconscious on the ground.

With something of a start, she realized that she could now see the faces of the men very clearly in her mind. Somehow, in her near-unconscious state, their faces registered in her mind, and as she closed her eyes she was able to recall their leering faces leaning over her, one by one. She shivered, wondering how she had been able to avoid being raped, and then decided not to dwell on *that* anymore. They must have been in a hurry. Be thankful for small favors.

She wrapped the blanket around her more tightly and decided to try and get some sleep. In the morning she and Blossom would start walking — at as slow a pace as the horse required — and hopefully they would reach a town before they both dropped from exhaustion.

CHAPTER TWO

Liz was three hours on the road before she found the man. Or rather, the remains of what had once been a man.

She ground-tied Blossom and then proceeded cautiously to the atrocity before her.

They'd worked the man over with more than a little pleasure. He had been stripped to the waist, lashed to a pine, and then flayed with a whip.

Liz had never seen anything like it. The gashes were so deep in his chest and arms that she thought she could see white bone. They had even whipped his skull. Tufts of hair had actually been torn away.

At first the young blonde woman could only stand and take terrible measure of the man's condition. She assumed he was dead, but then she heard a faint, horrible rattle in his throat. On the still morning air it sounded like something from the grave.

When he looked up, she almost jumped. His eyes were ghoulishly white in his blood-smeared face. She shook herself then, realizing that she now had work to do.

Behind this stand of pines ran a creek, glistening in the bright morning sun. She went to its banks, ripped off a corner of her blouse, and soaked the material in the clean, clear water.

By the time she got back to the man, his head was slumped down again and his eyes were closed. She spent ten minutes washing him, making two additional trips to the creek to resoak the material.

"Can you speak?" she asked him at one point.

Nothing. No response whatsoever.

"Can you speak?" she asked again, speaking louder the second time.

This time the head stirred slightly and the eyelids fluttered faintly. Then with what seemed to be a monumental effort, he raised his head and opened his mouth.

And she almost wished he hadn't.

A sound came from his mouth like none she had ever heard before. She saw the bloody stump of his tongue and realized that someone had cut more than half of it away.

She took a moment to recover from the shock — not from the man's condition, but that there was actually someone who could have done something this horrible to another human being. She went back to administering to him and was so engrossed that she did not hear the man emerge from the dense pines a few hundred yards to the north.

Beefy, somewhat handsome despite his bulk, and

wearing a worsted business suit too warm for the day, he knelt on one knee and leveled a Winchester at her. With slicked-down hair and walrus mustache, he might have been a sporting-club member out shooting quail.

In truth, he was out shooting Angels.

The first shot missed Liz but caught Blossom in the shank, felling the horse.

Angel Eyes, seeing what had happened to her beloved bay, thought not of her own safety but of preventing any further harm to the animal.

That was when the kneeling man fired his second shot. Had Liz not been moving toward Blossom the shot might have been a more telling, perhaps even fatal one. As it was, the bullet creased her at the temple. She fell with the same terrible finality that Blossom had.

Then, for the second time in fourteen hours, darkness claimed her.

She awoke a few minutes later to the clatter of a dozen or so wagons being pulled by a score of horses.

Her head throbbed and the noise sounded to her like thunder, only coming from inside her head. When she put her fingers to her face, they came away sticky and red with blood. She had been lucky. The bullet had traced a path along her flesh and kept going without causing serious injury. Depending on how you looked at it, she had either been very unfortunate over the past fourteen hours or extraordinarily lucky.

A glance at Blossom told her that the felled mare had not been quite so lucky.

She was kneeling by the horse, examining the flank where the bullet had punched through the flesh, when the caravan of wagons pulled up. Obviously, it had been the sound of the approaching wagons that had driven off Liz's assailant before he could finish the job.

By now she had ascertained that the mare's injury was not life threatening, though the horse would certainly be in pain and a long time healing. The wound was right on the joint of the front right flank. Walking would be difficult, running impossible, but the mare would be able to travel.

"Easy, girl," she crooned to the skittish, confused horse. "You're going to be just fine."

When she turned to look back at the wagons on the road, she had the impression that she was seven years old again, a pretty little girl in pigtails and a gingham dress and missing a front tooth, laying eyes for the very first time on the wonders of a circus.

Captain Barnaby's Traveling Wild West And Theater Show was several rungs below a legitimate circus, of course. Its wagons were muddy and old, almost as old as the tired horses pulling them; the paintings on the side of the wagons advertising the show were silly, lurid depictions of a lone white man slaughtering what seemed like hundreds of near-naked Indians; and the people on the seats of the wagons looked just as worn as their vehicles. Without the mercy of makeup, they were older than they appeared in performance. Only one person that she could see was young and vibrant, a lovely dark-haired woman who stood impatiently with her hands on her hips, having stepped down from her wagon.

She wore a plain skirt and blouse, but the way she wore them might have made you think they were expensive finery. She had full, heavy breasts and a trim waist which made them seem even larger. She was tall, perhaps a couple of inches taller than Liz, and she was darkly beautiful. She had long, very black hair held back from her face with a bandanna, and very dark eyebrows over large brown eyes. Her full mouth was set in a straight line now, as she obviously was not happy about the delay.

From the first wagon a man stepped wearily down. He had flowing blonde hair and the fancy mustache of George Armstrong Custer. He wore an Edwardian coat and a fancy vest. As he approached with a somewhat uncertain gait, she could see that he was at least a little drunk. He was probably no more than fifty, but years of rotgut whiskey and hard living had left his pallor and his gaze with the aspect of a living corpse. He came over and stood above Liz, and she thought that she had never seen such sad eyes.

The man regarded her for a moment and then lifted his eyes and looked at the man lashed to the pine. For a moment she thought he was going to faint, and at the very least he had suddenly become cold sober.

"My God!" the man said in a much richer baritone than she would have expected. "It's Johnny Shilstone!"

CHAPTER THREE

For the next two hours, they worked on the man who had been lashed to the tree.

She now knew the drunken man as the Captain Barnaby whose name was on the wagons, and she watched with surprise as his long-fingered, liver-spotted hands worked calmly and capably cleaning and binding the man's wounds.

They had raised him gently into the captain's wagon, where he now lay on an unmade cot. Liz looked around the interior of the wagon. The walls were covered with mementos of a career spent in the lower echelons of the dramatic arts. Only one faded poster, depicting a young Barnaby handsome almost beyond recognition, proved that at least for a time his career had been promising. According to the poster, he had played the lead in *Hamlet* at the famed Salt Lake City Theater.

He must have practiced medicine somewhere along the line too, she thought as Captain Barnaby finished up his work with the man he'd called Johnny Shilstone. He worked with fascinating competence, considering the condition he'd apparently been in when she first saw him. Ironically, now that Johnny Shilstone was bathed and his wounds cleansed, he looked even worse. The cuts were that fierce, the effect that devastating.

Liz decided it was time to check on Blossom and left the wagon. She'd forgotten what a beautiful day it had started out to be. The May sunlight kissed the lodgepole pines lining the road she'd been traveling, and in the distance the rimming mountains were a soft blue. This was the prettiest part of Nevada she had seen.

The people of the carnival caravan had made camp and watched her closely as she made her way to where Blossom stood resting. For some reason they depressed her. Maybe it was the sullen gaze in their eyes for a stranger, an outsider. She had heard stories about these people, carnies, gypsies, stories that said they were all thieves — and worse.

They were a curious-looking lot, to say the least. One was a nearly seven-foot Indian wearing an eye patch over his left eye, and the others included a plump woman in Annie Oakley garb, a chunky man with a shaved head, and a lean, handsome man she had not noticed earlier. He too wore an Edwardian coat, but she was more interested in the dual lowslung Colts he wore on his hips.

Behind them others completed the odd picture: an old gent with flowing white hair and a buckskin coat, a Kewpie-doll-cute white girl, and a midget who held a huge, black cigar between his pudgy fingers as he eyed Angel with obvious, almost exaggerated lasciviousness.

She was aware of all their eyes as she inspected Blossom's wound. She saw that someone had packed the wound well with balm and covered it with enough gauze to absorb the drainage.

Suddenly a huge cloud of cigar smoke engulfed her and caused her to gag.

Coughing, she looked around and then down to see the midget, dressed up in the three-piece suit of a banker, standing close by. He tilted his black derby hat back with a fat thumb and regarded her with a gaze she was hard put to determine. He had brown eyes like muddy puddles and a snub nose. When he grinned, she could see that he had teeth missing. There was a certain amount of mischief, and what appeared to be a touch of malice. She had never seen a midget up close before and was afraid that she might have been staring.

"You know what you should do, don't you, lady?" he asked. His voice was deeper than she would have guessed.

"What's that?"

She tried to keep her voice neutral to disguise the fact that the little man unnerved her.

The man smirked and said, "Well, what do you think? What do they always do to wounded horses?"

She knew what he meant and didn't like it. She had never agreed with the practice of shooting wounded animals instead of trying to save them, and the suggestion that she should do that to Blossom made her angry.

"I don't know," she said, dropping her hand down

next to her gun. "What do they do to wounded midgets with warped senses of humor?"

For the first time the midget seemed to see her as more than just a lady he could aggravate.

"Hey," he said, holding his hands out, palms forward to ward her off, "I was just trying to be helpful. I didn't mean no harm."

"I don't need that kind of help, thank you."

He surprised her then by extending the hand that did not hold the cigar for her to shake. She took it and found it board-hard.

"My name's Edgar. Ain't that a hell of a moniker for a midget?"

"Glad to meet you, Edgar," she lied.

The little man had suddenly become charming, and she found that she liked that even less.

"Sorry I stepped out of line." He nodded to Blossom and said, "That's actually a beautiful animal."

"Yes, she is."

"Is Edgar giving you any trouble, miss?" a male voice asked.

When she saw the duded-up gunslinger walk over, she was impressed with two things — his dark good looks and his graceful way of moving. Then she noticed something else about the man. His right hand was bandaged from the wrist down.

The gunslinger dropped his left hand to Edgar's shoulder and smiled.

"Don't let him fool you," the man said with an easy, attractive grin. "He tries to be a mean little guy, but he's actually a disgusting little pervert."

"You flatter me," Edgar said with a quick grin.

Liz had the impression that the banter was normal for the two men, who seemed to be friends.

"I'm William J. Quick," the dark man said, doffing his flat-crowned Stetson.

"Pleased to meet you," she replied. "I'm Elizabeth Archer."

"He's better known as Billy Quick," Edgar said. "At least he was until he fell down and hurt his wrist. Now we call him Clumsy and Quick."

The little man cackled.

"If you don't pipe down, I'm going to take back all the nice things I said about you," Billy Quick said, squeezing the little man's shoulders.

Liz nodded toward Quick's hand and asked, "Well, at least part of what he says seems to be true."

"Oh, I sprained my hand, there's no doubt about that," the man said, raising it so she could have a better look at the injury. "I just didn't happen to do it where and how Edgar says I did."

"Which is?"

"Jumping out of some back window while the husband was coming in the front," Edgar added quickly, cackling gleefully again.

Billy Quick flushed, and Liz had the feeling that the little man had touched a sore spot.

Then the little man said, "Well, wherever you did it, it's costing us a lot of money."

"Why's that?" Liz asked.

Edgar nodded to the tall man.

"This here is the indisputable star of Captain Barnaby's whole show. The best gun handler in the West." Edgar was speaking now as if he were up on a soapbox, playing to a crowd. "When he sprains his hand, Captain Barnaby's Wild West show loses a lot of income. The ladies don't want to see their idol unable to shoot.''

"He *is* wearing two guns," she pointed out.

"Let me tell you about *that* —" Edgar said enthusiastically.

"Forget it, Egar," Bill said tightly.

Liz thought that the banter might be getting out of hand now, with each trying to outdo the other in front of a stranger.

"Hell," Edgar went on, "even worse than that, old Billy here didn't get a chance to kill Elmore Purvis."

Liz had heard of Elmore Purvis, of course. He was the noted — or notorious — gunman who had a rep for a quick and steady hand, a sharp eye — and no nerves.

"You were going to face Purvis?" she asked Billy.

"He sure was," Edgar said, proud of his friend now, "but then he went and sprained his hand."

From the look on Billy Quick's face, Liz thought that spraining his hand might have been the best thing to happen to him in a while.

Before she had time to speak, the sound of a single shot roared through the little camp.

Screams sounded and feet slapped the hard ground, running in the direction of the shot.

Liz, Billy Quick, and Edgar followed the crowd to the wagon where the blast had come from — Captain Barnaby's.

CHAPTER FOUR

The acrid smell of gun smoke wafted from the wagon by the time the trio reached it.

In addition to the carnies she'd seen before, Liz now saw the beautiful, dark woman she had noticed earlier and a boyishly attractive man with an unlikely shock of gray hair who she was seeing for the first time.

Without thinking, Angel Eyes drew her gun and moved nearer to the wagon. The carnies stared at her. They were not accustomed to seeing an attractive woman wearing a gun and handling it as confidently as she was.

"Are you all right, Captain Barnaby?" she called out, edging closer still.

No answer, just the sounds of the day. Birds. Some small animal digging in the distance. A chittering squirrel.

Angel Eyes eased the hammer back on her gun. She had no idea what had happened inside the wagon. She hoped no one noticed how her hand trembled. She wasn't afraid. It was just the proximity of death. It always reminded her of what the Nolans had done to her family and fiancé.

Suddenly the flap on the wagon was thrown back and there stood Captain Barnaby, looking glum and shaking his wrist.

"How about getting up here and giving me a hand?" he asked Liz.

To the rest of his troupe he said, "Everything's all right, people. We've got a fair piece of traveling to do before the show tonight. Let's get these wagons moving out." He looked at Edgar and said, "Why don't you walk the lady's horse — very carefully, you understand?"

Edgar smiled and nodded.

Liz put up her gun and climbed into the wagon with the captain's assistance. Inside, she found Johnny Shilstone covered by a sheen of perspiration that she could smell. He looked haunted, as if he'd literally seen a ghost.

"Tried to shoot me," Barnaby said, shaking his head. "Can you believe that?"

Liz moved closer to the wounded man.

"Where did he get the gun?"

"It's mine," Barnaby said. "He picked it up off the floor."

Liz got down on one knee next to the man.

"Johnny? Johnny, can you hear me?"

She felt as if she were shouting down a very deep well. He was in shock and not at all responsive. There was a good possibility he wasn't hearing her at all.

"Johnny?" she said again. "Captain Barnaby and I are here to help you."

He gave no sign of responding. He just lay there, staring wide-eyed at the wall.

Liz was extending a gentle hand toward Johnny when she noticed a slip of paper on the floor by the cot. She picked it up, smoothed it out, and examined it.

It contained a single, raggedly scrawled two-word phrase:

"Red wagon."

"What's that?" Barnaby asked.

"I don't know," she said. "Maybe you can tell me. Is it yours?"

Barnaby took it, looked it over, and shook his head.

"He must've written it."

"Any idea what it means?"

"None," he said, handing it back.

She held the slip of paper up in front of Johnny's staring eyes.

"Did you write this, Johnny?"

His eyes suddenly grew wider. His teeth began to chatter. Obviously, the phrase "red wagon" meant something to him.

"Would you write out what it means?"

His eyes began to dart around the wagon, as if seeking some sort of escape.

"Maybe we'd best leave him alone for now, miss," Barnaby said softly.

Liz glanced up at him, and realized that he was right. She was so intent on finding out who had done this to Johnny, and to herself and Blossom, that she'd been pushing the wounded man too hard.

She stood up and swayed dizzily.

"Maybe you better let me take care of you now," Barnaby said, putting out a hand to steady her.

"Yes," she agreed, "maybe you should."

"Sit here."

He helped her to a stool and then bent over to study her wound. She could smell his sweat and the liquor on his breath.

"It's not bad," he said. "I'll clean it up for you. You'll have a headache for a few days."

"That's all right," she said. "It will go with the rest of my aches." Her body still ached from being thrown by Blossom the day before.

"Are you a doctor?" she asked.

"Not hardly, miss. I've just patched up a lot of people in my time."

As he worked on her wound, Liz said, "You mentioned a show tonight."

"Yes, in the next town."

"May I travel with you?"

Captain Barnaby studied her for a moment. He still looked like a slightly degenerate theater man with long blonde hair and a wrinkled, somewhat aristocratic face, but there was now a hard, sober intelligence in his eyes.

"You're looking for something, aren't you, young lady?" he asked.

"Of course," she said. "I want to find whoever flogged this poor man and shot me and my horse." In addition, she related to him the incident of the day before, when she'd been attacked and robbed by the six riders.

"Vengeance is a heavy load for one so young to carry, especially a woman."

"I'm not unaccustomed to carrying it," she said, standing up. "I'll manage."

His eyes continued to assess her.

"You're quite a paradox, you know. So beautiful, yet as ruthless as any man, I'd wager."

"When circumstances warrant it."

"Well, you're welcome to ride with us for as long as you like," Barnaby said. "Do you have any ideas about who might have done it?"

"I don't know," she said. "I don't know Johnny Shilstone at all. Did he have any enemies, maybe members of your troupe?"

Captain Barnaby paled — if it was possible for an incredibly pale man to do so.

"You think someone in the troupe did this to Johnny?"

She shrugged. "I don't know what to think. I don't know the people involved. I suppose it's a possibility."

He shook his head.

"What's going on here?" he asked quietly, talking to himself.

Liz touched his arm.

"Let me ride with you a few days, Captain, and see what I can find out?"

"I already said you were welcome. Are you going to be asking a lot of questions?"

"Some, and I'd probably start with you."

"Me?"

She nodded.

"Why was Johnny riding ahead of the troupe?"

He shrugged.

"I don't know. All I can figure out is that he snuck out to meet someone during the night — and then this happened to him. We got a late start this morning. He wasn't all that far ahead of us, a couple of miles at most."

"You didn't notice anything strange in your camp last night?"

"Like what?"

"A fight, an argument?"

"No, nothing like that — " he began, then stopped and said, "Oh, just the usual banter that goes on between carny people, but nothing like what you mean."

Liz looked over at Johnny Shilstone. He was unconscious again. His breathing was ragged, his mouth open. He needed a doctor badly, and she wondered if he'd make it to the next town alive.

"I guess that's all my questions for now, Captain. I know you'd like to get under way."

Barnaby smiled wanly and said, "After this is over, you can write to Mr. Allan Pinkerton and tell him you want to sign on as one of his agents."

She smiled back.

"That doesn't sound like such a bad idea."

CHAPTER FIVE

The rest of the dusty afternoon was spent trailing just behind the slow-moving caravan as it made its way toward the town of Skyview.

Blossom neighed in pain occasionally and walked with almost comic stiffness, but in general she seemed to be doing well enough, considering her bullet wound was less than six hours old. The injury to her front hoof now seemed negligible.

The troupe amused Liz from time to time by taking up a few bawdy songs which they belted out with all the fervor of dance-hall ladies on a Friday night.

Every once in a while the midget Edgar or Billy Quick would come back to spend a few flirtatious minutes, pretending to see if there was anything they could do for her.

She liked the innocence of their attention; it put her in mind of barn dances on moonlit nights, when the scrubbed young men of the valley would tend to her with bows and grins and eager looks.

But then the dust of the road choked her and she was drawn back to the present.

Around three, Barnaby called the troupe to a halt.

Nearby was a creek. Liz walked Blossom over to it, gave the mare some water to drink and washed her down some, then did the same to herself.

The countryside here interested her. The new spring made everything an eye-stunning green. She decided to ground-tie Blossom and go for a short walk along the creek bed.

Her five-minute sojourn was just what she needed to put herself in a better frame of mind. She saw a doe, a cardinal, and about the cutest wild puppy she'd ever laid eyes on but could get nowhere near.

Reluctantly, hearing Captain Barnaby's voice in the distance calling the wagons to roll again, she went back to the bank where Blossom waited.

Ten yards from her horse she stopped short and stared. The man with the gray hair and youthful face she'd seen earlier was there, going quickly through her saddlebags.

He took things out, studied them, and then put them back. He was so busy with his thievery that he didn't hear her come up behind him.

"I didn't want to believe the stories," she said to let him know she was there.

He stiffened momentarily, then relaxed and asked, "What stories?"

"About carnies being thieves."

"They're not."

"You could have fooled me. Take your gun out

with your thumb and forefinger and drop it on the ground.''

"It'll get wet.''

"Toss it away from you, then.''

He did as he was told.

"Now turn around.''

He turned and looked surprised at the fact that her gun was still holstered. She was struck again at the unlikely combination of a young face and the gray hair.

"I want you to put back everything you took.''

"I didn't take anything.''

"I don't believe you.''

He grinned, enhancing his boyish look.

"What would I take? Some nice lace underthings? I'm a man, lady. You don't have anything I want — not in your saddlebags, anyway.''

"Then why were you going through my things?''

"I just needed to check you out is all.''

"Check me out?''

He nodded.

"For what?''

"To see who you really are.''

"Why?''

"Because it's my job.''

"You're not making much sense, mister.''

"If you'll allow me to reach into my back pocket, I think I can fix that for you.''

She hesitated, then nodded.

He took out his wallet and handed it over to her.

"Open it.''

She did.

The first thing she thought of was the joke Captain

Barnaby had made some hours before, about her joining the Pinkertons. The man standing in front of her was, according to his identification, John Cody.

He *was* a Pinkerton agent!

"I don't have the time to explain right now," he said, "because they're moving the wagons out, but you can trust me to tell you everything tonight. All right?"

She handed him his wallet back.

"I'll listen to what you have to say," she said, "and then I'll decide if I'm going to trust you."

John Cody grinned and said, "That's fair enough."

CHAPTER SIX

The transformation stunned Liz.

A couple of hours later she stood on the edge of a meadow on the north edge of Skyview and watched, along with at least a dozen or so scruffy local kids, as a group of weary and dirty carnies became a magical troupe of cowboys and Indians, heroes and villains.

A three-piece combo began playing melodramatic "Indian" music as Captain Barnaby entered the meadow astride a huge white horse. Barnaby wore the buckskin and white hat associated with the dime-novel heroes. He rode over to where about a hundred people had gathered by now and addressed them.

"If you would be so kind," he said, using his best baritone theater voice, "as to allow us to entertain you, we will show you delights beyond your imaginings."

Liz thought that he sounded like a whorehouse hawker.

With that, Edgar, dressed as an Indian, doffed his derby — to which he had added a feather — and began taking up a collection.

At first the locals, mostly married couples and sweethearts, seemed reluctant to part with their money, but one man, a red-faced, prosperous-looking businessman, made a display of dropping a gold eagle into Edgar's hat, and soon the others followed, putting in whatever they could afford.

Seeing how the proceedings were going, Barnaby guided his horse to the center of the meadow where virtually everyone with the troupe was dressed up as a cavalryman or an Indian. Only the women stayed in ordinary clothes, though they were heavily made up.

In his deep, resonant voice, Barnaby said, "I do what I do because it is my duty to my country, to my manhood, and to the Great Spirit."

Just then the chunky, bald-headed man Liz had seen earlier — who she had since learned was a fire-eater — stepped up with a megaphone and announced, "Ladies and gentlemen and kids of all ages, you are about to see the most thrilling, most realistic, most heart-pounding, most authentic wild West show ever staged for your pleasure and edification. Let the show begin!"

And so it did.

Liz had once seen the fabled Tompkins Wild West show, and while this, with maybe a fraction of the number of actors, was no match for the more famous show, it did have an energy she would not have expected.

The citizens of Skyview fanned out in order to see the show better. Because neither the town nor Captain Barnaby could afford to erect bleachers, they would have a long period of standing ahead of them, but they obviously did not mind.

The festivities started with the plump Annie Oakley, here called Annie Lee Todd, doing some very fancy trick riding. Then came the fire-eater, named Tony Higgins, who walked up to the seven-foot Indian with the black eye patch — was it on the other eye now? — and took a blazing torch from his hand. The Indian made a great display of being shocked at what happened next — Tony Higgins put the flaming torch down his throat! The audience went berserk with appreciation.

The beautiful dark-haired woman was next. Introduced as Magda, she sang three lovely, melancholy songs. Her eyes never once left the face of the gunslinger, Billy Quick. Her love for the man was obvious.

The cute little girl with the Cupid's-bow lips was next. Evangeline Hart. She sang two "naughty, bawdy" ditties in a tiny voice. You could feel the women in the audience stiffen. Equally, you could feel the men stirring. The combination of her innocent beauty and bawdy songs was working its magic on the male populace.

Then Captain Barnaby rode in, firing a rifle, startling everyone.

"I am told that there are enemies of the Republic in our midst tonight!" he shouted. The way he rode in, so abruptly, and the sharp report of his weapon gave his performance more effect. The audience couldn't be sure if he was acting or not, which was exactly what Barnaby wanted, of course.

"I am your enemy!" screamed the seven-foot Indian. He drew a bowie knife and lunged for the captain.

The cowboy-and-Indian part of the show — with virtually everyone shooting, stabbing, and dying — had begun in earnest.

Liz, amused to see the Pinkerton John Cody playing an Indian, folded her arms across her chest and watched with pleasure.

CHAPTER SEVEN

Ernest McCarthy, a big man in a three-piece worsted suit who was sporting a walrus mustache that he took care of obsessively, entered the Skyview saloon with a look of disgust on his arrogant, handsome face. The tin cans used for urinals didn't get emptied as often as they should have, and the floor was chunky with last night's vomit. He wrinkled his nose, but approached the bar.

It had not been a good past two days for McCarthy. He had not gotten the information he had wanted out of Johnny Shilstone, and then he had not been able to finish off the woman who had interrupted him. Now he was here, in a saloon that would disgust pigs. He had been "out West" for six years now and had not yet been able to get used to some of the conditions he found in these western towns.

The bartender, who had contempt for eastern

dudes, knew enough not to misjudge this man. Dude or not, there was a look of barely contained rage in the big man's eyes.

"I want a new bottle, unopened," McCarthy demanded. "I don't want any liquor that your filthy hands have come near."

"Yes sir."

For the next half hour McCarthy sat at a table near the player piano. If he closed his eyes as he listened to the music, he could almost imagine himself back in Boston. He thought of large, plump white breasts perfumed just so. If he had not been implicated in an unfortunate case of embezzlement, he would still *be* in Boston, enjoying the finest women and all the other pleasures of civilization.

As if to remind him of his fallen condition, the sour smell of urine wafted over to him.

He bunched his fist and slammed it hard against the table.

The handful of men in the place looked over at him and then quickly away as he gazed at them malevolently, daring them to say something. A couple of them found reasons to leave and did so. This amused McCarthy. He liked it when people were afraid of him. Smart people were afraid of him. If anyone had any doubts, all they had to do was ask Johnny Shilstone. But no, they couldn't ask Shilstone because the man had no tongue with which to answer.

McCarthy had hacked it out with a knife, and that memory made him smile.

The image of Shilstone, blood gushing from his mouth, his eyes wide with pain, unable to move because he was lashed to a tree, remained with McCarthy and amused him.

Unfortunately, he hadn't gotten what he wanted, what he needed from the man. He had heard the soft nickering of an approaching horse and had hidden and watched the young woman tending to Shilstone. Finally he'd decided to get her out of the way. He'd felled her with a shot, but before he could check to see if she was dead, there came the sound of approaching wagons. He'd been forced to leave the area without satisfaction.

Oh, to be in Boston . . . .

Occasionally, he could hear the sounds of the wild West show on the edge of town. Many of Skyview's people were there, and many more would go.

As Ernest McCarthy did now.

CHAPTER EIGHT

Billy Quick was the last act to take the center arena as dusk began to fall.

He was all tricked up, looking almost like a parody of a gunfighter. This particular set of Edwardian clothes had fringes on the coat.

Liz was surprised to see him try to perform. How could he do trick shooting with an injured hand — unless he used his left? As the men had responded to Evangeline Hart and Magda, so the women swooned over Billy Quick.

He was strikingly handsome, no doubt about that, as he strode to take his mark.

Edgar, having discarded his Indian getup, set up bottles on a fence for Billy to hit.

The crowd was ready.

Billy, using his injured hand, missed nearly every shot. Liz could only surmise that he wore the left gun for show.

The crowd responded curiously. They began to laugh at Billy Quick as if he were doing a comedy act.

Billy tried again.

And missed.

And the crowd laughed, but their laughter was becoming harsh, as if they had begun to suspect that something was being put over on them.

"I can shoot better than that!" shouted an obviously drunken townsman.

"Yeah, well, so can my six-year-old daughter," another man answered.

Billy, head hung low, obviously favoring his hand, took his place for one more try.

Angel Eyes saw that she would have to act quickly.

She found a large pine to hide behind. In the dusty light she just might be able to pull it off.

Billy raised his weapon, ready to fire. As he did, Angel Eyes fired with him.

A glass bottle shattered as if exploded from the inside.

The crowd gasped, fell silent, and watched curiously.

And so it went.

Using her unerring instinct, Angel Eyes fired with Billy Quick, their two shots mingling to sound as one.

Glass bottles shattered.

Plates, thrown into the air by little Edgar, exploded.

Edgar put a long stogie in his mouth, and Billy Quick appeared to cut it in half. The crowd applauded vigorously, now convinced that the real trick shoot had finally begun.

When it was over, they applauded Billy Quick, and not one of them noticed the frown on the man's face.

Captain Barnaby was once again astride his white steed. This time, as a closer, the entire troupe stood around Barnaby and led the townspeople in several choruses of patriotic songs.

Liz thought the finale was particularly clever and was singing along when she felt an arm slide around her waist. On the periphery of her vision, John Cody's face formed, smiling. She wanted to resent his touch, but she didn't. She found it very pleasurable.

"Why don't you move your arm?" she suggested.

As much as she might have enjoyed it, she did resent his manner and attitude, holding her as if she were his property.

Cody squeezed her tighter.

She put an expert elbow into his ribs, and the air whooshed out of his lungs.

"I would have thought the Pinkertons would have trained you better than that."

Rubbing his ribs, he grinned at her and said, "You could be dangerous."

"I am dangerous."

"Good. It gives us some common ground on which to build our relationship."

"Oh. Are we going to have a relationship?"

"Come on," he said. "I see the way you look at me."

"Do you mean the contempt or the amusement?"

"Pure lust, ma'am. Admit it."

They were standing near a stand of pines, apart from the rest of the show.

"I thought you were going to tell me why you were traveling with this show," she reminded him, changing the subject.

"I thought we could discuss that . . . after."

"After what?"

"After we both do what we've been wanting to do since we first saw each other."

"You're a confident bastard, aren't you?"

He grinned and said, "I just know my women."

"Then I suggest you go and find one of them," Liz said, turning on her heel. "Come and find me when you want to talk."

McCarthy had cut a whore once in Boston. Oh, he hadn't killed her, but he'd taken a pound of flesh out of her. He had never forgotten that sensation, the pure pleasure, the feeling of power, the whore's fear, her willingness to do anything he wanted.

McCarthy was thinking about this as he stood on the fringes of the crowd, watching the finale of the wild West show, watching the people disperse, head back to their ranches and sod huts and ramshackle little houses.

He was in a melancholy mood now, his belly warmed by whiskey, his thoughts of better times. He was getting older, and the more of life he saw, the less of it made sense. You lived and you died, and who knew what lay beyond the grave? You had to get all of the pleasure out of life that you could.

He felt the knife he kept in a sheath inside his pants. He knew the edge was keen, and it was still stained with Johnny Shilstone's blood.

He looked over at the wagons of the Wild West show drawn together in a semicircle.

He would be paying them a nocturnal visit later.

And he would be the only one to realize any pleasure from it.

CHAPTER NINE

Torches lit the night.

The gaudy illustration of the Old West on the side of the wagons seemed to come alive in the flickering light. Here a fierce Indian brandished a tomahawk or a knife, there a maiden cowered for her virtue and her life.

In the camp a kind of party was in progress. A stocky man with a concertina played happy songs to the delight of his co-workers while Evangeline Hart danced to his rhythms — to the delight of every man in camp.

Liz Archer stood on the periphery of all this, feeling shy about joining in the festivities. She had been examined by a doctor, and Blossom by a vet, who had removed the bullet.

"This is an especially sound and strong animal," he had said. "Given enough rest, she'll be fine."

Much the same had been said about her by the town doctor, who was a young enough man to have been impressed by her.

From behind her a baritone voice said, "I don't suppose you'd do the same thing tomorrow night."

As resonant as the voice was, there was something wrong with it.

Its owner was drunk.

Captain Barnaby came out of the shadows, not bothering to try and hide the pint of rotgut he was holding. With his makeup removed, he looked old and haggard.

"You saved the show tonight."

"I just wanted to help."

"You must have been shooting since you were a little girl."

"No," she said. Bitterly, she recalled how she had strapped on a gun for the first time after the Nolans had killed her loved ones. Tate Gilmore had taught her how to use it and had said that she was the most naturally gifted person he'd ever seen with a gun.

Had that only been — what, two years ago?

"Then you just practice a lot."

She shrugged.

He came up even with her and watched the young woman dance in the fiery circle between the wagons.

"They're all good, every last one of them."

"Yes, they are."

After watching them all in the show tonight, she had come to respect their talents.

"But without Billy Quick we'd never get a crowd."

"He's that important?"

Captain Barnaby seemed shocked.

"That important? Why, he's this poor excuse for a show's version of a leading man. He's young, he's handsome, and he's the only real crowd pleaser we've got."

"How did he hurt his wrist?"

Captain Barnaby hesitated, then said, "Before tonight I wasn't sure he really had."

"What do you mean?"

With that, Captain Barnaby tilted back his head and poured enough whiskey down his throat to amaze Liz.

After wiping his mouth on his sleeve, he said, "Never mind. Look, I'm going to make you an offer."

"What kind of offer?"

"If you back Billy up the way you did tonight, I'll pay you ten dollars a day."

She could have used the money, since she'd been robbed of all of hers, but she didn't want to break Captain Barnaby. She knew that paying her ten dollars a day would put a strain on him, and he had enough problems that were pushing him deeper into a bottle every day.

She put out her hand and said, "You've got a deal, Captain, but you don't have to pay me."

"Well, that's not right —"

"You've helped me out, and you're helping me by letting me travel with you. I want to help you."

"You're sure?"

"I'm sure."

He shook her hand and said, "Done." Showing her the bottle, he asked, "Drink?"

"No, thanks."

The captain stared at her then for a long moment, and she thought that he wanted to say something else to her.

"Well, good night then."

"Good night."

He turned and weaved back to his wagon.

When she turned back to the festivities, she saw that Magda — who might or might not have been a gypsy, though she was billed as one — had taken Evangeline Hart's place.

Magda cast a spell over the men in the camp that was quite different from Evangeline's. Her gorgeous body, in its peasant blouse and skirt, spoke of Central Europe, of dark secrets and old legends. In her flashing eyes was knowledge of other worlds. Liz could easily imagine the woman holding someone in thrall with her crystal-ball act.

As if to complement these thoughts, a wolf in the lonely distance howled at the full moon. Magda smiled, seemingly pleased at the vulpine accompaniment.

Abruptly, the festivities came to an end. The carnies in the circle all stood up with complaints of bad backs, of sleepless nights, of a hundred of age's infirmities. This was not an easy life, and it left them in constant pain of one kind or another. So now it was early to bed so they could rise early and move on.

Liz had decided to check on Blossom before turning in when someone said, "Excuse me a minute?"

Magda had come over to see her.

After a rather formal introduction, Magda said, "I believe you can help me."

"I'd be happy to, if I can."

"You may not be happy after you have heard my request."

"Well, let's hear it anyway," Liz said with a smile and a frown.

"You are a beautiful woman."

"Coming from someone as stunning as you, that's a great compliment, Magda. Thank you."

"And that is how you can help me," Magda went on, "with your great beauty."

"I'm afraid I don't follow you."

"I love Billy Quick."

"I see."

Did Magda think that she was after her man? Was she about to warn her off?

"Since Billy has . . . injured his hand, all he does is feel sorry for himself." The dark-haired woman leaned in and said in a whisper, "He is not even as good a lover as he was. He seems to have lost interest."

Liz wasn't sure she wanted to hear about Billy and Magda's sex life.

"Uh, Magda —"

"I have embarrassed you. I'm sorry."

"It's all right, Magda. Tell me, how is it you want me to help you?"

"I want you to sleep with my man."

"What?"

"He needs his self-confidence back. He needs to feel that he is desirable. If you would go to him, ask him to make love to you —"

"Magda —"

"I've embarrassed you again."

"You must admit this is a pretty strange request for one woman to make of another."

"I am confident of Billy's love for me or I would not ask."

"I see."

"You don't have to answer me tonight. You will be traveling with us. Just keep my request in mind, and if the situation arises and you want to help . . ."

"All right, Magda. I'll keep it in mind."

"Thank you. Good night."

"Good night."

She watched Magda disappear into the gloom between the wagons. She was about to go to Blossom when she heard a sound from near one of the wagons. Captain Barnaby had removed Johnny Shilstone from his wagon and put the injured man in his own, and it was this wagon she thought she heard the noise from. She approached it and saw a shadow.

"Who's there?"

From the darkness the little man, Edgar, came, smiling his disarming smile.

"I was just wondering if you needed anything, ma'am."

Even in the shadows it was easy to see that Edgar was lying.

"What are you doing near Johnny Shilstone's wagon?"

"Johnny's a friend of mine. I wanted to see if he needed anything."

"Real helpful little fella, aren't you?"

"It's part of my charm."

"Move away from the wagon."

Edgar did as she said, and she moved to the wagon and peered inside. She could hear Shilstone's tortured breathing but could not tell whether the man was awake or asleep. When she turned away, Edgar was gone.

Had the little man been inside the wagon, or had she heard him before he'd had that chance? And why would he be in the wagon bothering Shilstone, with the latter in such bad condition?

After checking Blossom, she walked to the wagon Captain Barnaby had indicated she would sleep in. Inside, three ladies lay sleeping. Annie Lee Todd, the plump one, was snoring lightly, and Angel recognized Evangeline Hart. She didn't know the third woman by name yet.

She climbed in, found the bed that had been prepared for her, and lay down without removing her gun.

Twenty minutes after the last lantern went out, Ernest McCarthy made his way into camp, his walrus mustache twitching with excitement.

CHAPTER TEN

Liz awoke, chilled with sweat from a dream whose details she could not recall.

She left the wagon, careful not to awaken any of her mates, and as she stepped down to the ground an arm came around her neck and a hand clamped over her mouth.

She did not have a chance to cry out.

Whenever he closed his eyes at the right moment, just when the alcohol made him peaceful as nothing else could, Captain Barnaby could bring back his wife.

Literally.

There before his eyes she ran in summer meadows, girl and woman both, friend and lover. He saw her on opening nights, her hair done up, a tiara flattering her blondeness. He saw her in the shadows of their bed, impossibly beautiful. Then he saw her on her final day . . . young and beautiful, but with a heart ailment taking all her strength. All he could think of — melodramatically, he admitted — were Edgar Allan Poe's poems about lovely women who died so young.

Then his eyes opened. He was no longer in a reverie. He was an old bastard, sauced up most of his waking moments, here in a rickety wagon in the middle of nowhere, begging dullards for pennies to support the illusion that he was still a man of the theater.

As if to confirm all of this, he raised the pint bottle — which he refilled endlessly from a vat that sat below three layers of shawls nearby — and finished it off.

He pushed himself to his feet abruptly, unsteadily, and staggered to the back of the wagon for some air. He stuck his head outside in time to receive a blow. . . .

Liz stomped on the man's instep with her heel and then grabbed his hair. She was about to smash his head into the wagon — *that* would wake up the women inside for sure — when moonlight fell on his face and she got a glimpse of a grinning mouth.

John Cody, the Pinkerton man.

"Why you —" she began.

"Scared you, didn't I?"

"Damn right you did!"

He put a finger to his lips, shushing her.

"What did you think you were doing?"

"Taking you away."

"For what?"

"What do you think?"

"You've got your nerve."

"I've got my lust."

"You —"

He stepped close to her and kissed her roughly.

"I want you, Liz."

It had been weeks since she'd been with a man, and her lips tingled from the kiss.

She didn't resist when he took her hand and led her away from the wagon, away from the camp. When they were far enough away, he slid his arms around her and pulled her close. He kissed her again and she kissed back, her mouth open, her tongue searching. She felt him open her shirt and slide a hand inside and caught her breath as his palm brushed her nipples.

"God," he breathed heavily.

They leaned back as one to the ground, quickly divesting themselves of their clothes. His hand went between her legs to the moist patch of pubic hair, and when his thumb brushed her clit she moaned and reached for his cock.

His hot mouth found her breasts, kissed and nibbled them into searing life. He raised himself above her, and she held him until the head of his penis prodded her moistness. She opened her legs wide, and he entered her fully, causing them both to moan. The Pinkerton skillfully found a rhythm they could both share, short thrusts followed by long, delicious ones.

Suddenly, he slid his hands beneath her and grabbed her buttocks, pushing himself into her deeply.

"God," she moaned.

She was almost over the edge when he slid himself out of her and put his mouth to her. He began to lap at her in such a frenzy that she thought she would lose her mind. She couldn't count how many times she achieved orgasm, thrusting her pelvis up against the pressure of his tongue.

Finally he mounted her again, plunged into her, and rode her had until they both cried out and came together.

They fell against each other, sweat drenched, chilled by the night breeze, so utterly spent that they might have fallen asleep that way — but for the scream that rent the air.

CHAPTER ELEVEN

Knocking Captain Barnaby out had been no trouble for McCarthy. He did it with his usual savage expertise.

Then he climbed into Shilstone's wagon and started working on the injured man.

McCarthy could see that Shilstone recognized him. That was good. That would only make his work that much more enjoyable.

He knelt next to the cot and put his hands around Shilstone's throat.

"I would've killed you if that blonde bitch hadn't come walking along," he whispered. "Now I can finish the job."

Shilstone's eyes threatened to pop out of his head. He tried to crawl backward up the canvas side of the wagon, but it did not good. McCarthy kept the pressure on his throat unrelentingly.

Then McCarthy slapped him.

"Where is it, you little bastard? Where is it?"

Shilstone just shook his head. Blood leaked from his mouth as the blow started his tongue stump bleeding again.

This time McCarthy took out his knife. He held it up in a shaft of moonlight so Shilstone could get a good, long look at it.

"You remember this, don't you, Johnny boy? It's the one I used on your tongue." McCarthy smiled and said, "Now I'm going to ask you one more time. Where is it?"

Shilstone shook his head. He was slick with perspiration.

McCarthy brought up the knife.

Shilstone just watched, frozen with fear.

McCarthy put the knife point just at the top of Shilstone's chest and then brought it downward, as if he were gutting a fish. Blood seeped from the shallow opening, then began to drip down. If McCarthy had applied a little more pressure, Shilstone *would* have been gutted.

Shilstone, horrified at what was happening, tried to form some words but could not.

"Somebody in this caravan knows where it is, don't they?" McCarthy asked. "You've got an accomplice, don't you?"

The beefy man was becoming angrier as he spoke. He thought of some of the people he had seen Shilstone with.

"Who is it, Johnny boy? The big Indian? The midget? The fire-eater? One of your cronies knows, doesn't he?"

Blood soaked into Shilstone's shirt and dripped down onto the cot. The man was incapable of answer-

ing now, McCarthy saw. He was going into a paralyz-
ed shock.

He was no good to him at all.

Outside, McCarthy heard Captain Barnaby moan
in the next wagon, and he knew he was finished here.

Taking Shilstone by the hair, he raised the man's
head up, exposing his throat, and wrenched his knife
from one side to the other, almost severing the man's
head.

Tomorrow, he thought, jumping down from the
wagon, he'd have to start on Shilstone's friends.

Ten minutes later the scream that alerted Liz and
John Cody also woke the entire camp.

At the creek bed McCarthy washed Johnny
Shilstone's sticky blood off his hands and shoes. He
smiled to himself as he watched the blood drip from
his hands. Blood gave him a sense of power.

He was looking forward to the next day.

More blood.

More power.

Twenty minutes after the scream, the butchered remains of Johnny Shilstone lay on a stretcher in front
of Captain Barnaby's wagon. A red-soaked sheet
covered him.

Everybody in the troupe was awake. They all had a
look of shock on their faces. Some were frightened by
the savagery, some angered, but they were all shocked.

Liz and John Cody stood on the periphery of the
camp, watching what was going on as the torchlight
faded into the dawning sky.

Liz excused herself briefly and went over to Captain Barnaby. The man was sitting on a huge rock, rubbing his face again and again, trying to waken himself from this nightmare.

"Do you know what happened?"

He looked at her, the misery he was feeling plain on his face, and shook his head.

"No, I don't know." He was holding his pint bottle and now surprised her by smashing it to shards on the rock. "When you live inside a bottle, you don't know anything but the bottle."

She put a hand on his shoulder to try and soothe him.

"It wasn't your fault."

"Maybe not, but then again maybe it was. Who can say what would have happened if I'd been sober for once?"

"So you really don't know what happened?"

"As near as I can recall, I put my head out of my wagon for some air and somebody tried to take it off. I don't remember anything else until Vangy screamed."

It had been Evangeline Hart who had discovered the body of Shilstone. What she was doing at the man's wagon no one knew.

Someone came up beside them and said, in a soft voice, "I'll look after him."

It was Magda.

Liz nodded and walked back over to where John Cody stood.

"Now I want you to tell me what's going on here," she said.

CHAPTER TWELVE

"Shilstone was a front for a gang of bank robbers."

"A front? What do you mean?"

"Well, you never saw him when he was all spruced up. He was a good-looking man and a very crafty one. That's why Captain Barnaby used him as a greeter for his show."

"What did that have to do with him throwing in with bank robbers?"

"Well, think about it a minute. A charming man can get a lot of information that others can't. That's what Johnny Shilstone did. You can take a map and follow Captain Barnaby's troupe across a six-state area. In their wake were a dozen bank jobs, each of which looked like some kind of inside job. They weren't, though, not exactly. What happened was that Johnny Shilstone struck up a romance with a female who worked in each bank and learned everything he possibly could. Then he passed the information along to the people he worked for.''

"Do you know who they are?"

"Not really. All I know for sure is that the gang's leader is a man from the East who's wanted in several states for a variety of crimes — a man named McCarthy who nobody seems to know. There's no photograph of him, for instance, and whatever posters are out on him have no drawings. However, one of the gang was shot in a saloon in Wyoming and talked about McCarthy. He sounds like a very bad man. Shilstone couldn't get all the information McCarthy wanted from a woman named Betty Sims, so McCarthy took over himself. He mutilated the woman.''

Liz thought of how Johnny Shilstone's tongue had been cut out, and shuddered.

"The gang's biggest job was a bank in Denver," Cody went on. "It so happened that the bank was storing very large bills directly from a federal agency at the time. They got away with nearly one hundred thousand dollars.

"It was never recovered?"

"No. That's why I'm here. An association of bankers hired us to find out what's been going on. I was just about to close in on Shilstone when he wandered away from the caravan yesterday morning and got himself carved up — probably by McCarthy.''

"So now you have to find McCarthy?"

"Yes, McCarthy and Johnny's accomplice here in camp.''

"His accomplice?"

"I'm sure he had one. Shilstone was the kind of man who couldn't keep a secret. The thief who died in the saloon in Wyoming told us that McCarthy had gotten very angry at Shilstone because Johnny said that he'd told somebody in this troupe everything, as a kind of insurance. Now I've got to find that person before McCarthy does.''

"That's means that somebody in this camp —''

Nodding, Cody finished the sentence for her.

"— might know where the money is. As near as I can figure, that's what this is all about. Shilstone must have double-crossed McCarthy, taken the money and hid it somewhere. That's why McCarthy tortured him, only Johnny must not have talked and McCarthy came back tonight to finish the job.''

"Do you think he knows where the money is now?''

"I don't think so. I don't think he had time, and he probably killed Johnny just for spite.''

"And now he's got to find Johnny's accomplice.''

"Right, and I sure wouldn't want to be that person if McCarthy gets to them before I do.''

"Do you think Johnny's accomplice knows what McCarthy looks like?''

"I doubt it. That person wasn't really part of the gang.''

"You keep saying 'that person.' ''

Cody shrugged and said, "It could just as well be a woman as a man.''

Liz decided to tell Cody what she'd found in the captain's wagon that morning, next to Shilstone's cot.

"We found a piece of paper with the words 'Red wagon' written on it. They might have been written by Shilstone. Does that mean anything to you?''

Cody thought for a moment, frowning, then said, "No, I can't say it does. Maybe he was delirious.''

"Maybe, but for some reason I don't think so."

"Do you have any ideas what it could mean?"

"Not just yet, but I'm going to start asking questions about it."

"You plan on doing my job for me?"

"I'm going to help you."

"Find McCarthy?"

"Yes?"

"And the money?"

"Yes, but you can have the money. McCarthy shot both me and Blossom and tortured poor Johnny. I want to see him pay for all of it."

"I'm sure you could make him."

"Why do you say that?"

"Oh, maybe it's that orange bandanna you wear tucked into your collar all the time."

"What about it?" she asked, her hand flying to her throat to finger the bandanna.

"I've heard stories about a beautiful blonde woman who wears such a bandanna."

"What have you heard?"

"That she took her vengeance on some men for killing her family and has been riding a rough trail ever since. That she's fast with a gun and not shy about using it when she has to."

"Sure you want to get involved with a woman like that?"

He grinned and said, "I already am."

Sometime later, after the local sheriff had been informed about what had happened and had removed the bloody corpse of Johnny Shilstone, Captain Barnaby's caravan moved on.

CHAPTER THIRTEEN

By the middle of the next morning, the caravan was pulling into a small town of false fronts and a played-out gold mine. The welcome sign listed 879 residents. Liz doubted that there were that many left.

The warm spring sunlight and the blue foothills nearby seemed to put the carnies in a better mood. The image of Johnny Shilstone was not quite gone, but it was fading.

Many of the women went to the main street to window-shop. Some of the men went to one of the three saloons.

Liz was washing down the bed of what had been Johnny Shilstone's wagon, trying to get the blood out, when Magda came by.

"I am afraid you won't be able to help me," the dark-haired woman said.

"Oh? Why is that?"

"You made Billy Quick angry."

Now that Magda mentioned it, Billy had been avoiding Liz ever since the show last evening.

"How?"

"You made a fool of him. He has no pride left at all now. Nothing."

"That's foolish."

"Men are foolish creatures."

Liz couldn't argue that.

"Magda, were you with Billy when he hurt his wrist?"

"No, he was alone."

"He was supposed to face Elmore Purvis, wasn't he?"

"Yes. Why?"

"Do you think there was any chance that Billy was afraid of that confrontation and either faked the injury or hurt himself on purpose?"

Magda flushed and said quickly, "Billy, afraid? Of course not."

Liz had the feeling the other woman was merely rushing to her man's defense.

"You're sure?"

"Of course I am!"

"Magda, I'm not calling Billy a coward. For the most part gunfighters like Elmore Purvis are bullies and drunkards. They are not people I look up to. It's to Billy's credit that he might not have wanted any part of that fight."

Tears glistened in Magda's eyes.

"It's very difficult for him, you know."

Liz waited for the woman to go on, feeling that she was about to open up and not wanting to break the mood.

"He is so fast and accurate with his gun, and he is so much the image of the classic gunman: the tall, slender body, the good looks, the clothes. Everyone assumes that he is a gunfighter . . . but he is terrified! That man Purvis is a crazy man! He tried to force Billy into a fight, but Billy . . ." Magda had to stop, for her tears were choking her.

"Magda, let me talk to Billy."

"He has no pride left."

"Let me talk to him and see what I can do."

"Don't tell him I told you," Magda said, frightened now.

"Of course not."

Magda grinned slightly and said, "You are my friend."

"And you are mine, all of you are. I want to help."

"Thank you," Magda said, and left.

Liz went back to her scrubbing, and soon all that was left of the previous night's violence was a pinkish stain in the wood.

CHAPTER FOURTEEN

The man seemed to come up from the heat-shimmering desert itself, almost a mirage at first, a fat, balding monk in brown robes with a weary-looking burro beneath him.

Earlier in the day, the townspeople had been busy watching the carnies for amusement. There was a sense of danger about the carnies, but in a town this small sometimes you were thankful for a sense of danger. It broke the monotony.

Now attention turned to the monk.

He rode down the main street with a nod to everyone who caught his eye. Two of his fingers were raised in a vague sort of blessing. His lips were parted in a smile, like flower petals opening.

Liz, who had come into town with Captain Barnaby after she finished cleaning Shilstone's wagon, paused on the board sidewalk with all of the others and watched the monk.

Most of them assumed that he must be a man who knew no fear, to be traveling the desert alone. Others thought he was just a fool.

The monk came to a stop at the Catholic church, dropped his big body to the ground, did some stretching to make his back feel better, and then went inside.

The townspeople and many of the carnies seemed disappointed. The show was over. Most went about their business as some waited to see when he would come out.

"You look like you could use some suds," a small, hard voice said behind Liz.

She turned and then looked down at the midget, Edgar.

Actually, his suggestion did not sound too bad.

"A lot of our people are in a saloon down the street. Why don't we join them?" he suggested further.

"Why not?"

There was no better way to find out information about Johnny Shilstone and his accomplice than by talking to people whose tongues were being loosened by liquor. In fact, maybe she'd buy a few rounds herself.

They made an odd couple, the beautiful blonde woman and the little midget who some might have called ugly. Other, kinder people might have simply called him unpleasant looking.

Onlookers grinned, some with malice, exchanging dirty looks and thinking dirty thoughts for their own amusement about what these two would look like in bed together.

The saloon was about what Liz expected. A long plank for a bar, two or three choices of hard liquor, and pails of beer on the counter.

The carnies had taken over one end of the place, more or less by default. As more of them moved to that side of the room, the townspeople just naturally gave it up and moved to the other. Both groups eyed each other suspiciously.

From what Liz could see, they had been drinking hard and fast, possibly to forget what had happened to Johnny Shilstone right in their midst.

Liz sat with Edgar, the midget, and Tony Higgins, the bald fire-eater, and Black Feather the Indian who, even seated, was as tall as many men.

Beer was brought in a bucket and poured by Tony Higgins into mugs. He'd already had enough beer and liquor, and his pouring was none too accurate. They were paying for a good portion of beer that was not even getting drunk. The table shone with small puddles of brew.

Higgins raised his mug and said, "How about a toast to Johnny, the poor bastard."

"Why?" Edgar asked.

"He was one of us," Higgins said.

"He was never one of us," Edgar said sourly. "He was just slumming."

"What do you mean?" Liz asked.

"He always thought he was better than us."

"That ain't right —" Higgins began, but Edgar cut him off angrily.

"Hell it ain't! Tell them, Black Feather."

"We were not . . . friendly," Black Feather said, and let it lie.

"I'll give him one thing, though," Edgar said. "He was good with the ladies. I saw a few good-looking women on the way over here. I'll bet that by now Johnny would have had two or three of their names."

"There was nobody better with women than he was," Tony Higgins agreed.

This made Liz stop and think. Was this the answer? Was Johnny's accomplice in the caravan a woman? And if so, who? Magda? Evangeline Hart? Or one of the others?

After they had absorbed more beer, Liz brought up the note Shilstone had written so she could see what the others thought.

"When Johnny was in Captain Barnaby's wagon, he wrote something on a slip of paper that didn't make any sense to us. Maybe it will to you."

"What was it?" Edgar asked. All three men leaned in, interested.

She took the note from her pocket and handed it over to Edgar.

He looked at it intently for a few seconds, then his features drew together in perplexity and he handed it to Black Feather.

The big Indian had the sort of face you saw on statues. A hawk nose jutted from a forehead of granite. Gray, intelligent eyes assessed you with impersonal interest. Black Feather's face was impossible to read as he handed the note to the fire-eater.

Tony Higgins put the note down without reading it and poured himself another sloppy beer. Somehow he managed to avoid getting the note wet. He took a big, healthy swallow and then slammed down his glass and picked up the note.

"I needed a little more of the suds for inspiration," he explained.

He squinted at the note. It was obvious that the man needed eyeglasses, but like most men, he was too vain to wear them. Liz watched his face carefully. For a moment she thought she saw something in his eyes, perhaps a glimmer of recognition, but then there was nothing. She had either made a mistake or he'd covered up very well.

"Red wagon," he muttered, "red wagon."

Finally he handed the note back to Liz, picked up his mug, and said, "Sorry. Doesn't mean a damned thing to me."

"Let me ask you something else then."

"What?" Edgar said.

"With Johnny being so popular with the ladies, did that extend to the women in the troupe as well?"

The three men exchanged glances, and then Edgar said, "Well, I guess you'd have to ask Vangy about that."

"Evangeline? Were she and Johnny . . . close?"

"Like I said," Edgar repeated, "you'll have to ask Vangy herself."

She was about to pursue the question further when she heard something from the next table that made her stop. Two gnarled old townsmen were sitting at the table playing pinochle when one of them, looking out the front window, spoke to the other.

"Well, thunderation. You ain't a-gonna believe who just came home."

"Willie, now you just sit down here and play cards,

you hear? Don't be telling me no stories to distract my attention.''

The other man, standing up now and peering outside, said, ''I ain't a-funnin' you, Chester. Guess who's back big as life and twice as ugly?''

''Your wife.''

''Uglier than that, even.''

''Who?''

''Old Emore Purvis, hisself.''

''Elmore Purvis? Lessee!''

Now it was the other man who leapt up from his seat and gawked out the window.

''Well, I'll be damned if it ain't!''

None of the conversation was lost on any of them at Liz's table.

Edgar was clearly happy.

''Well, hot damn!'' he said. ''Elmore Purvis. If he gives Billy some time to heal his hand, Purvis is a dead man!''

''Nobody can outshoot Billy,'' Tony Higgins agreed solemnly.

''That's a fight I'd like to see,'' Black Feather said.

Obviously, Liz thought, none of the three carnies knew Billy Quick as well as they thought they did. They didn't understand that being a good trick shot had nothing to do with facing another man with a gun.

Nothing at all.

As the two old men hurried back to their table, the batwing doors were thrown back and there was a stream of light and a silhouetted figure standing in the doorway.

There, like a messenger from hell, stood Elmore Purvis.

CHAPTER FIFTEEN

As Purvis entered the saloon, Liz saw that he was out-fitted entirely in black, complete with black Stetson. It was just the way he dressed, but he naturally suc-ceeded in being dramatic in a way that Billy Quick — who tried for it — failed to achieve.

Purvis said nothing to any of the greetings that were offered him by the admiring townspeople as he crossed to the bar.

He asked the bartender for the best whiskey he had.

"I'm afraid it's none too good, Mr. Purvis," the bartender said, as if he wanted to make sure that he didn't take the blame for it.

"Whatever it is, it'll do."

Liz could easily overhear the conversation because absolutely no one else in the place was talking.

Two things surprised her: Purvis's age and his apparent mild manner. Beneath the hat was a wind-ravaged face that put the man near forty. Most gunmen were in their late teens or early twenties. Presumably they either did not live to become older or gained wisdom with age and gave up such folly.

As for his demeanor, he might have been a farmer who had come in off his farm for a drink after plowing a field all morning. She had heard him described in the past as "a crazy man" and "a wild-eyed killer". Neither description fit the man she was looking at now.

Edgar leaned forward.

"I'm going back to camp to tell Billy that Purvis is here. He's going to be real happy."

Liz felt her stomach tighten up. She felt sorry for both Magda and Billy. The sudden appearance of Purvis was not good news.

Edgar hopped down from his seat and waved goodbye, then moved quickly, crablike, to the batwing doors.

A few minutes after he'd gone, Purvis turned to look at the people in the saloon. For a few of them, apparently townspeople for a very long time, he had an almost imperceptible nod. For others, just a hard, flat stare.

When his gaze fell on Liz Archer, however, he stopped, his eyes fixed.

A minute later he came over to the table, bringing his whisky bottle and two clean glasses.

He stood over Tony Higgins and Black Feather and said, "Why don't you two gentlemen let me sit alone with the lady and buy her a drink?"

They looked at Liz, who, not wanting to cause

trouble, nodded. Besides, she wanted to talk to Purvis.

The fire-eater and Indian stood up and moved to another table, and Purvis — who stood six-two — did not even blink at the Indian's height.

"Care for a shot of whiskey with your beer?" he asked Liz after they'd gone.

"No, but you go ahead."

He sat and studied her.

"You're one of the most beautiful women I've ever seen."

"Thank you."

"I can't believe you're a carny."

"As a matter of fact, I'm not."

"Then why are you with them?"

"I'm just traveling with them."

"Why?"

"I have my reasons."

"Private reasons?"

She nodded and said, "Private reasons."

"Most people answer my questions."

"Most people are afraid of you."

"And you're not?"

"Should I be?"

"Well, I haven't ever harmed a woman in my life — yet."

"That's an enviable record."

Purvis poured himself a drink and drank it down. Watching him, she thought she could sense the pent-up violence in the man and, looking into his eyes, she might have been able to catch a hint of the "crazy man" within.

Holding his empty shot glass in front of him and

studying it intently, he said, "There's a man with the carnies I'm looking for."

"Oh?"

"His name is William Quick. Billy Quick, they call him most of the time. Do you know him?"

"I know him. What do you want with him?"

"I want to kill him."

"Why?"

He looked at her then and smiled.

"I have my reasons."

"Private reasons?"

He hesitated, then put the glass down and said, "No, not really. I want to kill him because he killed my brother."

Talking about his dead brother seemed to upset the man. He picked up the whiskey bottle in his black-gloved hand and poured a drink. His hand was steady, too steady, as if he were fighting to keep it that way.

"My brother was sixteen years old. That was two years ago. This Captain Barnaby's wild West show came through town — this town — where the kid was an apprentice blacksmith. He saw Billy Quick do his trick-shooting act and decided he wanted to be just like him.

"So what did the kid do? He gave up his job and traveled around with the carnies so he could learn to be a trick shooter. Then one night in Dodge City he got liquored up and decided that trick shooting meant fast shooting. He challenged a second-rate gunman named Harry Doakes who needed another kill to add to his reputation. My kid brother called him out and Doakes murdered him."

"Was it a fair fight?"

"Fair? My kid brother was no gunman, lady. It was murder, pure and simple. He was murdered by two men. Harry Doakes — and Billy Quick."

"How could you blame Quick?"

"He filled my brother's head with nonsense about trick shooting. That kind of shooting is easy, anybody could do it. It takes guts, though, to face another man with a gun. My brother had that, at least, but it was all he had. Only, Billy Quick convinced him he had more."

"Sometimes you need to let things go, for your own peace of mind."

"I don't let things go, lady. I take care of them. I promised my ma and pa I'd watch out for the kid, make sure he didn't turn out like me. Now he's dead."

He drank the whiskey in his glass and poured another with the same steady hand. If the whiskey was fazing him, he didn't show it.

"It took me a long time to hunt Doakes down, but I found him and I killed him, gunned him in the street like a dog. Now I want Quick the same way."

He drained the glass and put it down.

"You go and tell Quick what I said. You tell him I want his cowardly ass in the street at three o'clock tomorrow."

"If his hand is healed."

He thought a moment.

"I'll give him two days then. If it isn't healed by then, I'll come for him anyway."

"What if the show pulls out?"

"He better stay behind and face me or I'll hunt him down."

"He didn't murder your brother, Purvis."

"I say he did."

Liz stood up. She noticed his eyes suddenly focus on her throat — on the orange bandanna — and she thought she saw recognition in them.

"You tell him he's going to be dead in two days time. Understand?"

Liz nodded, and instead of joining Tony Higgins and Black Feather at their table, she left.

She had to talk to Captain Barnaby.

CHAPTER SIXTEEN

"You're finally going to get your chance," Edgar said the moment Billy Quick called out for him to come in.

The midget was shocked by what he saw inside the wagon.

Two empty bottles of whiskey lay next to Billy's cot. The sharpshooter himself hadn't shaved, he lay in white long johns stained with dirt and sweat, and the stench that hovered over him was oppressive.

Billy had the back of his hand over his eyes, as if shielding them from some intense, bright light.

"What do you want, Edgar?"

"I got good news for you, Billy boy."

Billy laughed shortly, a laugh that turned into a harsh cough.

"I could use some good news."

"Elmore Purvis just rode into town."

There was no reaction.

"Did you hear what I said, boy? Purvis is here, in town. You're finally gonna get your chance to gun him down."

The hand slowly came away from Billy's eyes. He sat up so slowly that you might have suspected him of being in great pain.

"What did you say?"

"I said Elmore Purvis just rode into town," Edgar said impatiently. What was wrong with Billy anyway?

"I'll be goddamned," Billy said in a low voice. He was speaking to himself, as if Edgar weren't even present. "So it's finally going to happen."

"That's what I been trying to tell you!"

Billy looked at Edgar and said, "You get out of here, Edgar, and right now. You hear me? Get out!"

"Billy, I thought I was giving you good news. I was trying to help —"

"You heard what I said, you sawed-off little bastard! Get out!"

For emphasis, he picked up one of the empty bottles and threw it toward Edgar.

Edgar stood there staring at Billy like some dog who had just been kicked by its master, then turned and left. By that time Billy was again lying back on the cot with his hand over his eyes, and did not even notice the little man go.

"What the hell are we going to do now?" Captain Barnaby asked.

"I'm not sure yet," Liz replied.

Barnaby sat at the rolltop desk in his wagon, with Liz seated in a chair beside him.

"Is there a chance?" he asked her. "A chance that Billy could win?"

"I don't think so, Captain."

Barnaby looked at her then.

"Purvis will kill Billy with no problem. It's what he does. Billy shoots at bottles and plates. Purvis shoots at men — and kills them."

"Then what are we going to do?"

"I don't know."

Captain Barnaby sighed, looking very old. His eyes lifted to the poster of himself as a young man, and he shook his head.

"They say you get wiser as you get older, but I've just been getting more and more tired. Look at all this shit," he said, waving his arms to encompass all of the paraphernalia on the walls. "I don't even know why I keep all this junk."

"You care about Billy, don't you?"

He looked at her and said, "Yes, I do. I care for all my people. Now Johnny's dead, and Billy's next, and I don't know what to do."

Liz stood up, put her hand on Barnaby's shoulder, and said, "I'll try and come up with something."

At that moment, however, she didn't have a clue as to what it might be.

Back in the saloon Elmore Purvis sat at the table he had shared briefly with the beautiful blonde woman. He raised his head to peer out the window, and it was then he saw the monk.

The man was across the street at Foster's General Store, packing supplies on the back of his burro. Apparently the man was going on a trip.

Purvis kept staring, something bothering him . . . and then he had it.

He knew who the monk was.

He laughed then, and everyone in the room looked over at him as if he had just fired a shot. He stood up, still chuckling, his body shaking with mirth as he walked to the batwing doors and stepped outside.

CHAPTER SEVENTEEN

"I want it dark. I want to be sure you're getting a true reading."

Magda looked at Billy and she could have wept. He had gotten dressed, but he still reeked of a night's drinking. He had not done well with her in bed for the fourth night running, and so had taken refuge in the bottle — only, that wasn't all that was bothering him.

He reached up and violently drew the curtain across the back of the wagon.

"I want it dark so you can consult the ball again."

"Billy, I have told you about the ball."

"You know it works, damn you!"

"I'm not sure it works. On my love for you, Billy, I'm not sure."

"I need the truth, and the ball will give it to me."

Magda sighed. She could see it was no use. Some

nights before, while drunk, Billy had demanded that she produce her crystal ball the same way she did for all the hick townspeople, and look into his future.

What she had seen was so dire that she had been unable to keep the truth from her face.

And she had lied to him.

Now she looked into the ball again and saw the same thing.

"What is it?" Billy asked.

"I am not sure I'm reading it properly."

"Damn you, tell me!"

"There will come a man in black."

"Purvis."

"And one of you will die."

"Which one?"

"The other man," she said, once again telling a lie. "The other man will die."

"So it's true, then," he said. "I'm going to kill Purvis."

"Yes," she said, "yes, you are."

What she had seen in the ball was Billy Quick, dressed in black, dying in her arms, but she did the only thing she could do. She lied to give him confidence.

Maybe if he believed it himself, maybe he could change what she saw.

"Why don't you go to the creek and get cleaned up for dinner, Billy?"

"Yes," he said, looking down at himself and wrinkling his nose. "That's a damn good idea."

She watched him leave, and when he was gone the tears came. She sobbed, wondering again if she had done the right thing.

John Cody was standing by Blossom, checking the horse over, as Liz Archer approached. A feeling of tenderness overcame her. She joined them, stroked Blossom, and kissed Cody on the cheek.

"Now that's a habit I'd surely hate to see you break, ma'am."

"I thought perhaps we could go for a walk."

"A walk sounds like a fine idea," he said. He stroked Blossom and said, "She's doing fine."

"I know. She's strong."

"Like her mistress," he said, taking her hand. "Where would you like to walk to?"

"Oh, just someplace where we could be alone."

He grinned.

"That was just the destination I had in mind."

They found a place near a cool, running creek, and Liz stripped off her clothing while Cody watched. When she was naked, he did the same while she watched. The cool breeze hardened her nipples just as Cody's hands found her breasts and squeezed.

They fell to the ground together, and she took Cody's swollen rod into her hands and nuzzled her face against it. Opening her mouth, she took it inside and began to suck and lick it until Cody's hips were lifted off the ground and his hands were holding her head.

When she felt he could take no more, she mounted him and engulfed him. The length of him was buried inside of her, and she began to ride him while he sucked her breasts. She went slowly at first, and then increasingly faster until he was gasping for breath. He reached behind her to grip her buttocks and pull her tightly to him as he ejaculated inside her. His sperm seared her insides and she came, their bodies pressed as tightly together as possible so that he was as deep as he could go. . . .

Elmore Purvis was as good with a chew of tobacco as he was with his gun.

He put a stream of brown juice right next to the monk's wide, sandaled foot.

The monk, who had been packing his burro, raised his head and met the harsh stare of the gunman.

"You gonna give me a few words in Latin, padre?" Purvis asked sarcastically.

"My way is the Lord's way."

"What the hell's that mean?"

The monk grinned and said, "I'll be damned if I know."

I've made a decision," Barnaby told Liz.

"What is it?"

"We're pulling out."

"When?"

"Tonight, in the dark. We've got to put some distance between Purvis and us before he realizes we're gone. After that, he'll have to track us."

"He will, and he'll find us."

"Maybe by then we'll have something figured out."

"How is Billy going to feel about this?"

"This is my show. Billy will do as I say."

"I hope so."

When Barnaby told Billy about his decision, Billy

went along with it. He didn't care. Magda said that he was going to kill Purvis, and he didn't care if it was now or later. His hand was better now, but in a couple of days it would be even more improved.

By the time Purvis found them, he'd be ready.

The monk and Elmore Purvis rode through the center of town together. The monk looked around and saw a buxom prostitute standing in the entrance of the saloon.

"Let's go in there. She's got great tits."

"That'd look great," Purvis said. "The servant of God slobbering all over a big-titted whore."

"I need a woman, Purvis. I'm not kidding."

"After."

"Then I need a drink."

"That I can oblige you with, but listen to me good. Your monk disguise is going to come in real handy with those carnies, so we can't afford anybody realizing that you're not actually a man of God. Do I make myself clear?"

The monk stared at the gunman hard. Finally he nodded and said, "All right, Purvis, I understand, but *you* get this. Don't think that you're giving the orders here, because you're not. Got it?"

"Sure, sure, I understand," Purvis said smoothly. "Nobody gives the orders here, padre. We're partners, remember?"

"Right. Just remember," he said. "Don't kill Billy Quick until we've found what we want, because he might be the one to show us where it is."

Purvis made a face.

"I don't want him thinking he got away with anything."

"He didn't get away with anything, Purvis, and he isn't going to get away with anything — least of all what's mine."

"Ours," Purvis said. "What's ours. We're partners, remember?"

Yeah, the bogus monk thought, you go right on thinking that way.

CHAPTER EIGHTEEN

Late the next day the Wild West show pulled into a glen just outside the town of Weymouth, where a ten-year centennial was taking place.

Liz washed her underthings in the chill, clean water of a natural spring, liking the way it made her hands feel numb.

She let the things soak for a time, sitting on a rock and watching a nearby frog watch, in turn, some nearby tadpoles.

She could scarcely believe what she was feeling and was, in fact, doing her best to deny it.

Could she possibly be falling in love with the Pinkerton man, John Cody? And if that was true, what did it mean about her feelings for Tate Gilmore?

While she was pondering all of this, a shadow fell

across her. She looked up and saw Cody standing there.

"Mind if I sit down?" he asked.

"Be my guest."

"You know," he said, sitting on the ground next to her, "you'd bear fine children."

The statement was so unexpected it startled her.

"To bear children I'd have to be married."

He looked at her and said, "Maybe that's exactly what I have in mind."

She stared at him for a long moment, and before she could speak, he beat her to it.

"Don't say anything now, Liz. Just know that I love you and want to marry you when this is all over. Think about it, okay?"

She smiled as he took her hand, and said, "Okay."

It felt good to be back. It felt right and as natural as anything in life but sex, and it gave him back his sense of self.

Billy Quick set up another row of bottles and quickly shattered them without missing a shot. His hand — which he truly had injured accidentally — was fine now. That blonde bitch wouldn't have to do his shooting for him anymore.

Various members of the show had come out to watch him practice, and they applauded. They stood in a semicircle in the grass a few hundred yards from where the wagons were gathered, and there were a lot of relieved smiles.

The star of the show was back.

Liz was one of the onlookers, standing with Edgar,

Tony Higgins, Black Feather, and Captain Barnaby.

"He's all right now," Barnaby said.

"His hand healed fine," Tony Higgins said.

"Looks like he's put the little lady out of a job," Edgar the midget said.

"That's fine with me."

"Maybe not," Captain Barnaby said ominously.

"What do you mean?" Liz asked.

"I've been thinking what an act the two of you would make together."

"Together?"

"Billy works alone," Edgar was quick to point out.

"Or against each other," Captain Barnaby said. "Imagine a shooting contest between you and Billy. We could bill you as the Six-Gun Angel."

Liz studied the captain to see if he was teasing her, but apparently his choice of the word "Angel" was quite innocent.

"I don't think so, Captain."

"Why not?"

"He's just got his confidence back —"

"You think you can outshoot Billy?" Edgar asked in disbelief.

"I didn't say that."

"Then you just don't want to lose."

Liz looked at Edgar and said, "If that's what you want to think, fine. Excuse me."

She started to walk away and saw Magda coming toward her.

"Magda —"

"He is beautiful to watch, isn't he?" Magda asked.

Liz didn't know what to say, so she simply agreed.

"I have a feeling that now I will not need that favor I asked you for."

"I'm glad, Magda. "

"Now if you do me the favor I will be very angry."

Jesus, Liz thought, now she *is* warning me off.

"Don't worry, Magda. I have no interest in Billy."

"I am happy to hear that."

Liz went to check on Blossom again. The wound was healing quickly. The area around it was not nearly as sensitive.

Staying with the show, she had lost sight of her original intention, which was to find the six men who had robbed her. She probably could have left the show and made better time on her own, but then there was the problem of finding McCarthy, who had shot her and Blossom. Maybe she should decide on which ones she wanted to find the most.

As she went back to the wagons, she saw Captain Barnaby again. She hoped he wouldn't pitch his idea again. She had no desire to pit her skills against those of Billy Quick.

The captain had an armload of fliers, though, and spoke of them and not his idea.

"Taking these into town. Help drum up some business for tomorrow."

Tonight was a "layover," as the captain called it. No show. Everybody got time to rest and relax. Except Barnaby. Liz knew enough about business — any business — to know that a good boss rarely got any rest and relaxation.

For the first time Liz became aware that Captain Barnaby was drunk. He weaved slightly and his eyes had a sad, lost look. One night he had told Liz about his dead wife, and she understood now why he drank. She just wished he could find some other way to deal with his grief.

The captain nodded good-bye and set off for town. If he hadn't secreted a pint in his pocket, the walk would do him good.

When they came within sight of Weymouth, Elmore Purvis could no longer take the smell and the slowness of the burro.

He told the monk, "Get down."

"What?"

"Get down."

"Why?"

"That burro is driving me crazy. He smells, and he's too damn slow."

"He's all right."

"I said get down."

The monk looked at him and saw that Purvis had that crazy look in his eyes. The monk wasn't ready for a showdown with Purvis. He wasn't ready to kill the man yet.

He got down.

Purvis dismounted, walked over to the animal, and put the working end of his gun right next to one of the animal's eyes.

He pulled the trigger.

Half an hour later, with the monk walking, they found a ranch with a small rope corral, just outside of town. Purvis dismounted from his horse, went inside, and led a sorrel out.

"Get on it."

"You're really pushing your luck, Purvis."

"I said get on."

The monk knew enough not to argue.

For now, anyway.

He got on the sorrel.

Purvis and the monk rode the rest of the way to Weymouth.

There was a lot of work to be done tonight.

CHAPTER NINETEEN

Liz Archer and John Cody sat in the back of a restaurant where lamb chops were the specialty.

Following dinner, Cody lit a cigar.

"Maybe we should go outside," he suggested.

"Why?"

"That's where the excitement seems to be."

He nodded to the street, where people of all ages were packed together to watch tumbling balls of fireworks ride high in the sky and light up the night.

"The excitement's here," Liz said quietly. "With us."

Cody grinned.

"Guess I couldn't disagree with that."

The sourdough who ran the place came over. For an establishment that had at least some pretensions to eastern gentility, the old duffer should have cleaned himself up some before even beginning to worry about building a clientele.

Liz, catching a whiff of the old guy, said, "Maybe a stroll outdoors doesn't sound so bad after all."

"No, it doesn't, does it?" Cody laughed.

The best part of the centennial festivities was watching the kids, Liz thought.

Farm kids, as she herself once was. Fireworks and apple cider and staying up late were big events.

Liz and Cody, hand in hand, strolled down the street to where some of the carnies had gathered to watch the display. Evangeline Hart danced to the tune of a fiddle with a young townsman already smitten with her good looks.

Evangeline saw the couple and smiled to them. Then she turned her attention to devastating the young man she was with.

Near the train station an orator on a soapbox read Weymouth's history in a fine theatrical voice while a group of town ladies hummed patriotic songs in the background.

Liz and Cody strolled past to where a display of livestock was being loaded into carts. The night air was filled with the smell of manure.

Liz saw a small crowd of people staring at the ground on the far side of the depot. She pulled a reluctant Cody in that direction.

"Get the sheriff," a tart-voiced older woman said.

"This is disgraceful," somebody else said.

"Just what you'd expect from people like them," said yet another.

When they reached the group, Liz looked down to the ground. A switchman held a lantern to the face of the older man, who was obviously passed out, drunk.

It was Captain Barnaby.

Liz dropped Cody's hand and marched up to the group.

"He'll be all right. He's with us. Let us handle it."

One of the older women sneered at Liz and said, "You're one of those carny people, aren't you?"

"Yes, ma'am," Liz said, "and you're one of those hypocritical old town biddies, aren't you?"

"Well!"

"Please," Liz said to the switchman, "we can handle him."

"Well," the switchman said, rubbing his jaw, "I guess it's better for him to sober up with friends than in jail. Get him out of here before the sheriff shows up."

"Much obliged, mister," John Cody said, moving to Liz's side.

Together they got Captain Barnaby upright between them as the crowd of people broke up and faded away.

Liz reached inside the breast of the man's jacket, found the pint bottle, and smashed it against the edge of a building.

"What are you, the temperance type?" Cody asked wryly.

"When it comes to people who can't handle their liquor, or who don't know when to stop, I am."

"And what's Barnaby?"

"He doesn't know when to stop. He's trying to wipe out memories of the past."

"Aren't we all, but we all don't try to do it with liquor."

As they got the captain's feet moving, a note fell from one of his pockets, where it apparently had not been well enough secured. Liz figured that if she put it back in his pocket, he'd only lose it again, so she shoved it into hers.

They moved unsteadily back toward the noise of the main street.

"The town's in a good mood to be entertained," Cody said. "The Wild West show should do well tomorrow night."

"If the captain is in good enough shape to run it, it will."

"Oh, he'll run it, drunk or sober. I've seen him do it many times."

She looked over at the captain's face as they half dragged, half walked him, and she smiled sadly. She couldn't help it. She liked the old man very much.

"He'll be all right," she said, agreeing with Cody.

As they hit the main street, their progress slowed because of the crowds. At one point they passed·an alley where two men stood watching them, but they were too engrossed in what they were doing to notice.

They just kept walking.

CHAPTER TWENTY

Ernest McCarthy was getting tired of the monk's disguise.

The monk's robes had started to chafe his beefy body. The social constraints of the robes were even worse. He wanted to tear into a big-titted woman and fuck her all night. That was a difficult thing to do when one was parading around as a man of God.

His original idea for the robes had been as a way of infiltrating the Wild West show. Now he wished he hadn't come up with the plan. He was tired of it, itching for the sort of stealthy, violent action that had defined his life.

Now, as Elmore Purvis stood behind him, drawing steadily on a foul-smelling, black cheroot, McCarthy forgot about how the robes itched and how badly he needed a drink and a woman. He saw the beautiful blonde and the dead drunk pass by the alley, another man helping her hold the old man up.

"Well, I'll be damned."

"There you go again, padre. Swearing." Purvis clucked his tongue.

"The man with the blonde."

"If it's all the same to you, I'd rather watch the blonde than the man."

"If I was you, Purvis, I'd take a good look at the man."

"Why?"

"He's a Pinkerton."

"You sure?"

"Damn sure."

"How do you know?"

"He was tracking Johnny Shilstone and me for months. He figured out how we worked the bank robbery setups."

Purvis drew on his cheroot again. In the amber glow of the fiery tip, it was evident that he needed a shave.

"I think we should have a little fun with that Pinkerton man tonight, don't you, padre?"

"Yes, my son," McCarthy said, chuckling. "That sounds like a very good idea."

"We should give them a couple of hours to get bedded down." Purvis threw the cigar to the ground and crushed it out with the toe of his boot.

"He might even be able to help us find out where the money is stashed."

"He might at that," McCarthy said. "But whether he does or doesn't, he's a dead man before the night's out."

"Agreed. You stay here and I'll go across the street and get us a bottle. It'll get us primed for tonight."

"May the Lord go with you."

He watched Elmore Purvis cross the street. He was afraid of Purvis, of course, but it was a constructive fear. It insured that he would always be alert and careful around the man. They had orginally met six years earlier in Missouri as McCarthy had been working his way west from the Boston scandal. For six months they had joined forces, working a variety of scams. If there was any trouble, Purvis always managed to get them out of it with his gun. Then one night in a Montana town a deputy sheriff gave McCarthy some trouble and Purvis wasn't around. McCarthy strangled the man, learning that not only could he defend himself very well without Purvis around, but that he took abiding, almost shameful pleasure in it.

They had split up after that, but had recently met again and begun working the bank robberies with Shilstone.

McCarthy was well aware of the fact that Purvis would try and kill him when they found the money. He'd seen many examples of how Purvis ridded himself of unwanted partners.

Only this time there was going to be a surprise. This time McCarthy was going to get rid of Purvis.

He even had his method picked out, a slow torturous method that was going to be much fun to put into practice.

After they found the money.

He was tireless tonight.

Earlier, Billy Quick had spread Magda's legs and buried his face in her tangy splendor, licking and nibbling her into an ecstasy she could hardly stand.

Then he mounted her and began to ride her furiously. It was as if he'd never come, even though his cock was swollen to the point of bursting, even though his moans indicated that he was getting at least as much pleasure as she was.

His tongue lapped her luxuriant breasts, found the hollows of her neck, shoulders, armpits, while all the while his hands were clamped on her buttocks so he could join their bodies even more tightly.

When he finally did come, she had to clamp her hand over his mouth, else he would have awakened the whole camp. Her own cries had been no easier to hold back.

It was good having Billy Quick back as her lover.

When they finished, Billy lay back and stared out the end of the wagon at the stars.

"Will you tell Magda what you're thinking?"

He laughed.

"I thought gypsies were mind readers."

She tickled his scrotum.

"Tell me or your punishment will be very severe."

He writhed beneath her nails like a little boy. Tickling him was one of the worst things she could do to him, but tickling him there . . .

"All right," he said, "just stop tickling."

She stopped and waited.

"Johnny Shilstone's money."

"What?"

"That's what I was thinking about. What would you say if I told you I knew how to locate it?"

"I say you should tell Liz and Captain Barnaby."

"Liz Archer? Why would I tell her?"

"Because she has come here to clear up the matter

of Johnny Shilstone's death once and for all. And to find out who shot her and her horse.''

"She's just after the money, like everyone else.''

"I thought you liked her.''

"Like her? I can hardly stand her.''

Magda said nothing more about Liz.

"How do you know where the money is?''

"I don't *know*,'' Billy corrected her, "but I think I know who does.''

"Who?''

"Who used to hang around Shilstone when he was drunk and bragging about his women?''

Magda thought for a moment.

"Edgar.''

"Right, but there were two others as well.''

"Black Feather and Tony Higgins.''

"Right again.''

"But if they know where the money is, why do they not take it themselves?''

"Because they probably haven't got all the clues put together yet.''

"What clues?''

Billy smiled.

"You remember how Johnny liked to tease people?''

She snorted and said, "Do I remember? As if he didn't tease me enough!''

"Exactly. Well, one night a few nights before he died I heard him saying to Black Feather and Edgar, 'I'll bet you a virgin's cherry I know where a lot of money is hidden.' And Black Feather said, 'Where?' and Johnny just laughed and said, 'Where the red wagon sits.' ''

"But that doesn't make sense.''

"Sure it does — or it would if we had the other clues."

"What other clues?"

Billy sighed in exasperation and said, "He must have teased them with other clues, Magda. If they were smart enough, they could put them all together and find the money."

"So how will you find out where the money is?"

"By getting them drunk enough to talk about their buddy Johnny. Why, I'll bet they've already been thinking back, trying to reconstruct everything he might have said to them."

"Do you have any idea what he meant by what you overheard?"

"Not yet."

She put her head on his bicep and said, "And just what would you do with this fortune if it was to become yours?"

"Make somebody I care about very happy."

"Oh, Billy, I love you."

"I love you too, but I was talking about Evangeline Hart."

There was a split second when she didn't know that he was kidding her, and then she slapped him on the chest.

"If I ever catch you with that little girl . . . "

He reached for her, bringing her face down to his so he could kiss her deeply, then held her face in his hands.

"I love you, Magda. When I get that money, I will give us both the life we deserve — together."

But Magda was already thinking of what she had seen in her crystal ball.

"We could leave tonight, Billy. Right now."

He sat up, startled.

"Leave? What are you talking about?"

"Say it is a premonition I have had, but it would be better for us to leave."

"Are you talking about what you saw in the ball? Have you lied to me?"

"No, it's not that," she lied. "It is the money."

"What about it?"

"It scares me. It will not be good for us, Billy. Let's leave now, please."

Her heart was like a wild bird in her chest. Did he believe her?

"You're talking crazy, Magda."

He pushed her away angrily, stood up, pulled on his pants.

"I'm going to sleep in my wagon."

Before she could say anything he grabbed the rest of his clothes and jumped out of the wagon.

"Billy, please —"

"I'm going after that money, Magda, and if you don't want to leave here with me when I get it, maybe I will ask Evangeline Hart — or Liz Archer!"

She recoiled from the sting of his words, and he vanished into the thick black of the night.

CHAPTER TWENTY-ONE

"God, I'm tired."

"I thought we'd spend a little more time together tonight."

John Cody's grin told her what kind of "time" he had in mind.

She leaned over and kissed him.

"I'm afraid I really am tired."

They had taken Barnaby to his wagon, and Liz had tucked him in as if he were a child.

Now Liz and Cody stood on the edge of the vast prairie night. In the distance the dark shape of mountains loomed. Behind the two of them, in the center of the circle of wagons, a campfire sputtered, dying out.

She leaned against him. Her father, Chance Taker, Tate Gilmore — each man in her life had taught her something that had strengthened her as a person, as a woman. As she in turn had taught each of them something. Now she was in that process again, of teaching and learning, with this man, John Cody.

And she was enjoying it — but she did need her sleep.

"I'll have to say good night, John."

"All right, then," he said, kissing her gently. "Good night. Sleep well."

She watched him walk away and felt an odd sadness come over her.

What was bothering her?

In the wagon she shared with the other women, she lay down on her cot. The captain had offered her Johnny Shilstone's wagon, but she had turned it down. A couple of members of the troupe had taken it, though, which was probably best. That way it would cease being Johnny's wagon, always reminding them of what had happened to him.

She was just rolling over when she remembered the note that had dropped from Captain Barnaby's pocket. It was in her pocket now.

At first she thought of waiting until morning to read it, but curiosity got the better of her. She stood up and quietly left the wagon, approaching the dying campfire. She pulled the note out and read it by the combined meager firelight and waning moonlight.

It was very simple:

IF YOU WANT HALF OF JOHNNY SHILSTONE'S MONEY BE AT THE CREEK AT MIDNIGHT.

It was unsigned.

The writing was in a blunt pencil, obviously written

by someone who didn't write a great deal. The paper had once had some sort of food wrapped in it.

The creek.

Midnight.

It was almost midnight now.

She thought briefly of going back to the wagon and to sleep, but she knew what she had to do.

As he got older, Black Feather — whose real name was Tommy Moondog — became increasingly near-sighted, and nights like this — with less than a full moon — did not help any.

Just after eleven-thirty the huge Indian had made his way from the wagons down to the creek. He had to move slowly, carefully. In addition to his near-sightedness, he'd had too much whiskey tonight.

He wondered if Captain Barnaby was going to show up tonight. He hoped so. The captain was really the only white man Black Feather had ever truly trusted. Oh, he liked Edgar and Tony fine, but he *trusted* Barnaby, and the reason was simple.

"We're a lot alike," the captain had confided in him one drunken evening. "We're both outsiders. People dislike both of us, and that's what we have in common."

So Captain Barnaby was the logical man to turn to, given what Black Feather had found out today. Even though Johnny Shilstone had given Black Feather the clue a couple of weeks ago, only today had it occurred to the Indian what it really meant.

As he approached the creek, he noticed that there was some fog rolling about. On the far side of the water stood a deer.

Black Feather went up to the water. The first thing

he did was relieve himself. The second thing he did was blow his nose.

The third thing he did was die.

But not right away.

Five minutes earlier Ernest McCarthy, dressed now in his worsted suit, the monk's robes having been stashed in his saddlebags, stood with Elmore Purvis on the edge of the Wild West show's camp and watched as Black Feather made his way into the night and toward the creek.

Neither McCarthy nor Purvis had seen anything else remotely interesting during the fifteen minutes they'd been watching, so they decided to follow the big Indian.

Either the Indian was very drunk or he was blinder than a cave bat. Twice he almost walked into a tree and once he stumbled comically.

They followed him to the creek, hid behind a stand of trees, and watched.

"He's waiting for somebody," McCarthy said.

"Looks that way."

"Maybe we should ask him some questions before his meeting starts."

"Maybe we should."

Purvis's eyes dropped to McCarthy's hand and saw the knife he was holding. Purvis had never known anyone who took such pleasure in the pain of others. The man had changed a lot in six years.

"Let's go," McCarthy said.

McCarthy took him down easily.

As the beefy man struck him behind the knees

Black Feather hit the ground hard enough so that the area surrounding the creek seemed to shake.

McCarthy made only one mistake. He was slow in clamping his hand over the Indian's mouth once he had him down, and the man got off a strangled cry. After that, McCarthy got his knife to Black Feather's throat and the man remained silent.

McCarthy was behind Black Feather, on his feet while the Indian was on his knees, and he kept his knee in the bigger man's back. The knife was tight enough against his skin to draw a thin line of blood.

"Where's the money, redskin?"

The Indian stank of whiskey and sweat, and after a moment, McCarthy smelled urine.

The big man had wet himself.

"Johnny Shilstone's money — *my* money — where is it?"

"Not sure," Black Feather croaked.

McCarthy switched the tip of the knife to one of the Indian's nostrils and said, "One more time, Indian, and you better damn well *get* sure."

"Not . . . sure . . . but . . ."

Purvis looked away because he knew what was coming. He could imagine what it would feel like getting your nose ripped open like that.

McCarthy must have had his hand clamped over the Indian's mouth because all Purvis heard was a strangled scream. When he looked again, McCarthy's hand was drenched with blood, and so was the Indian's chest. The blood looked black in the dim moonlight.

To Purvis the Indian looked big enough to throw McCarthy off of him, but McCarthy was using his considerable weight and the knee in his captive's back to keep the other man off balance and helpless.

Now McCarthy grabbed the Indian's hair and pulled his face around so that it must have hurt his neck.

Looking into the Indian's face, he said, "You've got one more chance, Indian."

Black Feather looked up at McCarthy and did something that surprised the others.

He spat in McCarthy's face.

McCarthy, immediately enraged, brought the knife up, and before Purvis could call out for him to stop, he'd plunged the blade deep into the Indian's right eye.

The sound the Indian made was like nothing Purvis had ever heard before. He went for his gun, sure now that the people from the caravan would be coming along any second now.

CHAPTER TWENTY-TWO

Liz was on her way to the creek when she heard the scream. It took her a moment to get her bearings and decide that was where it was coming from.

From behind her she heard, "You better wait for us."

John Cody and Billy Quick suddenly flanked her, both with their guns drawn.

"Got any ideas what's going on?" Cody asked.

"No."

"It sounded terrible, like an animal."

"That was no animal," Cody said.

Together they ran through the thickening fog to the creek. Behind trails of cottony fog they saw water glistening. Tall, black trees lined both sides of the water. They were thick enough for a man to hide behind.

"Nothing," Cody said.

"Fan out, and be careful," Liz said.

It was Billy Quick who found Black Feather.

"Holy God, over here!"

The Indian had been dragged into some tall grass but was lying with his face in the water. Cody bent over the man and managed to roll him over. Liz could see clearly that the corpse had only one eye. The other was just a gaping, bloody socket.

"Jesus!" Billy Quick said.

"Looks like our killer is back in business again."

Billy Quick swallowed hard.

"Maybe we'd better get back to camp and tell everybody."

Liz could see that the hand with the gun in it was shaking.

Liz and Cody looked at each other. They both knew that the killer couldn't have gone far.

Suddenly they both heard a sound from the thicket, like a man moving around.

"What is it?" Billy asked.

"Shh!"

For a long moment the night closed in, seemed to grow even darker. All that could be heard was the gentle flow of the creek and the hammering of their hearts in their ears.

Whoever was out there was damn good.

Liz couldn't hear anything else.

One moment she stood there, gun in hand, waiting anxiously, and the next thing she knew something hit her on the back of the head.

She fell, fighting against the loss of consciousness.

Her gun hit the ground.

Ahead of her now, coming from the bushes, she saw Elmore Purvis.

"If there's anything I hate, it's a Pinkerton man," he said.

She watched in disbelief, unable to do anything because she had no control over her own body. Her mind shrieked at her, "Move!" but her body would not — could not — respond to the command.

Lying there helpless, she watched and realized two things very clearly.

First, Elmore Purvis obviously planned on shooting John Cody down; and second, Billy Quick was just as obviously frozen with fear. He wasn't going to do a damned thing to help Cody — but how could she condemn him when she could do nothing either?

Together, Billy Quick and John Cody might have been able to take Purvis, but alone the Pinkerton never had a chance. He was a detective, not a gunman.

Orange-red light spewed from the barrel of Purvis's gun, and she did not even think that she had heard the shot. Her hearing seemed to have left her.

Twice Purvis's gun spat, and she watched as almost in slow motion the two slugs impacted on Cody's chest. Purvis had outshot him clean — and the Pinkerton man's gun had already been drawn!

Liz, still fighting the black vortex that gathered around her, raised herself up onto her hands and tried to scream, but it was no use. It was like being trapped in a slow-motion nightmare.

She saw Billy Quick turn and run from Elmore Purvis, and Purvis laughed and let him go. Then the darkness closed in and she almost welcomed it, because it signaled the end of the nightmare.

Or the beginning of a new one.

CHAPTER TWENTY-THREE

In the morning there were documents to fill out at the sheriff's office in Weymouth. Afterward, Magda convinced Liz to stop with her at the church.

She prayed for the soul of John Cody.

On the second day, in the afternoon, while they were getting ready for the four-o'clock performance — "We have to work or we don't eat," Captain Barnaby had explained to her — Liz took Blossom for a long walk. The mare was improving, but Liz did not yet want to take the chance of riding her. Barnaby had canceled the performance the day after Cody's death, but he said they had to perform now and move on.

They walked near the edge of Weymouth. From her vantage point on a hill, Liz could see the goings-on in town. It was beginning to reflect the modern age. Telegraph poles lined the roadways like sentries. At the opposite end of town a different kind of pole stood, a chemically treated one, for electricity.

There was a breeze carrying spring on it, and Liz stopped at the iron gates that were her destination. It wasn't right that the apple blossoms should smell so beautiful. It was not right that the wild flowers should look so yellow in the long grass.

Several yards behind the gate stood a large, marble angel. Black, with a wingspread of many feet, feminine in every respect, there was something ominous about her.

Liz stood beneath the angel, looking up at the curious, immemorial expression on her face. The angel knew the secret of why man was born to suffer and die, but she would never share it with a mere mortal like Angel Eyes.

On a hill overlooking a small valley, Liz found the place where the service had been performed the day before. She knelt and touched her hand to the fresh dirt and said good-bye to John Cody, a man she would never know if she could have loved, and married.

Near the fence she found some roses. She gathered some of them up and carried them back to the plain, granite stone that marked John Cody's resting place.

She was leaning over to place the flowers right on the grave itself when a shadow that seemed to blot out the sky fell over her.

She looked up and saw in silhouette a large, fleshy man whose robes looked familiar.

She squinted and remembered.

The monk she'd seen some days earlier, the odd

religious man riding a much-too-small burro out of the desert.

"You grieve, my daughter."

"Yes."

He put out a hand to help her to her feet.

Now that she could see him closely, she had the same impression she'd had when she first saw him. For some reason she could not explain, he simply did not look like a religious man.

"I am Friar Malloy," the man said.

Liz only nodded.

"I have come to the graveyard to be with my friends."

Llz frowned, obviously not sure what he was talking about.

The monk smiled.

"I call the dead my friends because they put up with me." With a huge hand he indicated all the tombstones. "They don't find my conversation tedious or my girth offensive. I only wish the living were as kind."

"I'm here to say good-bye to someone who died."

"Someone close to you?"

"He could have been," she said, indicating John Cody's tombstone. "We never had a chance to find out."

The monk looked at the stone and said, "He was a young man. Only thirty-one."

"Yes."

"I can see he meant a lot to you."

"Yes."

"But you see," Friar Malloy said, "now that he is here, I have one more friend. That means that his death was not for nothing."

"I'm sorry, friar, I can't see it that way. He was killed unnecessarily. It's such a waste."

"Killed?"

"A man named Elmore Purvis shot him."

"Ah, I see. I've heard of this Purvis. They say he is a truly evil man."

"So they say."

"You are planning vengeance," he said in a tone that clearly scolded her.

"It is something I'm used to."

"My daughter, you must let God provide his own vengeance. In time the scales balance. He sees to that."

"I can't wait."

"What will you do when you find this man?"

"I'll kill him."

"He may kill you."

She shrugged.

"Do you need lodging until you leave?"

"No, thank you, I'm traveling with the Wild West show."

"What a coincidence," the man said. "That is where I'm headed. One of my missions is to provide comfort for performers who are away from home. They go too long without their loved ones, and without God. Perhaps we can go together?"

She looked back at the grave and said, "If you don't mind, I'd like to stay here a few moments more."

Friar Malloy nodded and said, "Yes, of course. To finish saying good-bye."

"Yes."

For the first time he touched her. He extended a meaty hand and touched her shoulder, and she had to surpress a shudder. What was it about the man that made him so . . . loathsome?

"I will see you on the road then, my daughter. And in the meantime I will ask the Virgin Mother to pray for your young man."

"Thank you."

"I am but God's servant on earth. Better that you thank the Lord Himself than me."

Liz nodded.

She watched the monk leave and then knelt down. The breeze came, and once again the apple blossoms came with it.

It wasn't right.

CHAPTER TWENTY-FOUR

"He's drunker than anyone has a right to be — even me," Captain Barnaby explained to Liz. "You'll have to go on by yourself, Liz."

"I don't mind."

"I'll introduce you as Six-Gun Angel."

"Fine," she said, although she felt that "Avenging Angel" might have better suited her mood.

"Where did you find him?" Barnaby asked, indicating Friar Malloy with a nod of his head.

Liz had caught up to Friar Malloy, expecting to find him astride his burro. Instead, he had been on foot, and she had walked with him.

"I didn't. He found me."

She explained.

"Well, carnies aren't real big on religion. They hate being preached to."

"He says it's his mission."

"Well, far be it for me to keep him from his mission. God knows, with what's been going on around here it can't hurt to have him around."

"I guess not. Would you like me to wear something special? I don't have much."

"Ask Vangy to get you one of Annie Lee's buckskin jackets. That should do it. Do you want to use Billy's guns? He's too drunk to protest."

"I'll use my own."

"Suit yourself."

As she made her way back to her wagon to find Evangeline Hart, she saw that the carnies still had the sad-eye out for her. It was embarrassing. They were watching her as if they expected her to melt or dissolve into a mass of tears. She had seen too much grief in her life to react in that manner.

She was walking past Magda's wagon when the gypsy woman almost flew out of it and grabbed her arm.

"Please," she said, "you must see him. He needs to talk to you."

Liz frowned.

She had been dreading this moment.

She did not hold Billy Quick responsible for John Cody's death. She could not blame the man for letting his cowardice overtake him. He was suffering enough, blaming himself, trying to live with it.

Even if he had been brave enough to throw down on Purvis, it wouldn't have saved Cody's life, and it might have cost him his.

"Please," Magda said, her eyes pleading.

Liz did not resist as the woman drew her into the wagon and then stayed outside.

She wanted to get this over with. She would tell Billy she didn't blame him and then let him deal with it himself.

The wagon stank like a flophouse. Sweat and booze mixed with tobacco and vomit and urine. Liz, trapped in the shadows of the wagon's interior, almost gagged.

"Magda said you wanted to see me, Billy."

She saw something move in the darkness, heard something stir on the cot.

"I need your forgiveness," Billy Quick said, his voice a dry rasp that she barely heard.

"You don't need my forgiveness, Billy, you need your own."

"I really am what I've always dreaded I was — a coward," he sobbed.

"If that's what you are, Billy, then deal with it."

"Don't hate me, please."

"I don't hate you."

"I know how much you loved him."

If Billy Quick knew how much Liz had loved John Cody, then he knew more than she did.

She didn't reply.

"Maybe if I hadn't run —"

"I don't think so, Billy. I don't think you or I could have saved Cody."

It was as if he hadn't heard her.

"I don't know what I'm going to do with my life. I'm such a joke, impressing the rubes with my guns."

"Your life will be whatever you make it, Billy. You have Magda —"

He was crying. She could not remember the last time she'd heard a man cry. The sound froze her, filled her with pity and contempt in equal parts. Crying was not the way he was going to deal with his problems. It had never solved hers in the past, and she had given it up.

"I'll square things with Purvis for both of us, Billy. Don't worry."

He kept on crying.

She didn't know how to deal with the situation, so she just kept talking.

"All I can figure out is that he wants Johnny Shilstone's money, and that's why he's hanging around here. Maybe he's even the one who shot me and Blossom, but I don't think so. What happened to Johnny wouldn't be Elmore Purvis's style. That money, though, that's going to keep him near us, and I'll get him sooner or later."

She stopped because suddenly he had stood up, unsteadily approaching her. She didn't know his intention until it was too late. By then his arms were around her and his face was buried in her shoulder. He clung to her like a terrified infant.

She did not have the courage to push him away, not even when she suddenly felt him responding to her femininity.

She thought of what Magda had once asked her to do.

Sleep with Billy Quick.

Ordinarily, she thought him attractive enough, in a slightly seedy way, but now . . .

"Help me," he whispered, his breath hot against her neck.

His hands began to move over her, and she wasn't quite sure what to do. Somehow he had managed to open her shirt and her left breast filled his hand, the nipple hardening against his palm. Incredibly, she felt her body responding to him. What was this all about?

Billy's other hand dropped to her thigh and began a slow upward trail to the warmth between her legs.

"I can do it," she heard him whisper, "I know I can."

He lowered his head.

His mouth fastened to her breast, sucking the nipple, flicking it with his tongue. She had a nervous, fluttery feeling in her stomach as his hand began to undo her pants.

"Please," he said into the valley between her breasts, "please . . ."

She allowed him to push her down onto the soiled cot. His hands were all over her, and he had her shirt completely off now, lying around her waist because it was still tucked into her pants.

His hot tongue was on her, licking her nipples, turning them to eager buds in spite of herself.

It was perverse, but she was extremely sexually excited, and she couldn't figure out why. Was it because Billy was using her body to purge his guilt, to make him feel like a man? Was it because she simply wanted sex, needed it now, to make her feel alive?

"Billy," she said, sliding her hands up beneath his shirt. His skin was hot and dry, like paper.

"Yes, I can do it," he was mumbling. "Please . . ."

He had her pants open now and his hand was delving inside, looking for the moist slit between her legs.

She closed her eyes as his fingers found her, as his mouth suckled her breasts. She thought about Johnny Cody, and then about Tate Gilmore.

He pulled her pants all the way down until he had worked one leg over her boot, then settled between her legs, moving his face to her fragrant pubic thatch. Incredibly, as soon as his tongue touched her she came. It was nothing earth-moving and she did not even think he was aware of it, but she was, because it seemed to drain all of the tension from her body.

Suddenly she wanted to get away from him. She felt guilt, and shame, and desire. . . .

He rose to his knees between her legs, pulled his pants down, and suddenly stopped.

"Shit."

She wasn't sure she'd heard him, but he said it again.

"Shit!"

"Billy . . ."

"Jesus Christ!" he said with vehemence.

"What's wrong?"

She looked into his eyes, and then down at his shame. She could smell him then and saw that he had soiled himself with his seed.

He pulled away from her, buried his face in his hands. On the heels of everything else that had happened to him, this was unbearable. He obviously felt that any hint of manliness he might have had left had been stripped from him by a single, uncontrollable act.

"It's all right, Billy, really."

She sat up and quickly began pulling her clothes on, suddenly acutely aware of Magda's presence outside the wagon. If she had walked in during the past few moments . . .

"It's not that important, Billy, really it isn't."

"I'm sorry," he said.

"Don't be —"

"I'd like to be alone now."

"Billy . . ." she said, reaching a hand out to touch him. He recoiled from her.

"Please."

"All right." Since it was obvious that she could do nothing to console him, she decided to leave him alone.

In truth, she'd done more harm than good for him, she thought as she left the wagon. Magda looked to her for some sort of comfort, but she found she couldn't look the woman in the eye.

"Liz —" Magda said.

"I . . . have to get ready for the show," she said, and hurried away.

CHAPTER TWENTY-FIVE

"And when taps are blown at nighttime," Captain Barnaby intoned, standing in the center of his Wild West show as nearly a hundred townspeople looked on for this, the second hour of the show, "when taps are blown at nighttime, it is believed that the ghosts of the fallen dead rise up to guide other settlers on their journey across the plains."

With that, a vignette began as the sad-sweet sounds of taps filled the late afternoon air.

Two carnies, dressed as a pioneer couple, stood several yards away from Captain Barnaby and looked around, as if fearing attack.

Sure enough, here came two more carnies, these dressed up in war paint, as Indians.

They attacked, knives reflecting the blood color of the sun.

At this point Evangeline Hart, dressed in gingham and looking more virginal than ever, ran out.

"Do not kill my parents! Do not kill my parents!" she cried out with melodramatic zeal.

One of the Indians, in response, grabbed Evangeline and proceeded, through broad implication, to hone his lusts for later on.

So went the Indian-attack portion of the show.

Half an hour later Angel Eyes was on the last trick of her shooting performance.

This required Edgar to stand on a box, put a long black cigar in his mouth, and let Angel Eyes — or Six-Gun Angel — shatter it in half with a bullet.

To make the event even more spectacular, the midget was dressed up in tie and tails.

He stood now, waiting.

"I wouldn't let no woman with a gun do that to me!" hollered a drunk from the crowd.

Laughter rippled through the onlookers, but their eyes were riveted to Liz, moving away only occasionally to look at Edgar.

Liz blew the cigar in half with one shot.

Then, as planned, cavalrymen and fake Indians rode into the stage area for the finale. The three-piece band went into a medley of patriotic songs.

Tony Higgins rode past Liz. She had never seen him perform this particular stunt before. On horseback he put flaming torches down his throat. The crowd applauded appropriately.

Liz went to the far end of the staging area and found Blossom just where she had left her. This would be the first time she'd tried to ride the horse

since they were both shot. At first the mare shied
away nervously, but Liz spoke to her, calmed her,
and then mounted up.

Now they rode in wide circles along with the rest of
the troupe, and for the moment Liz got caught up in
it. She didn't think of Johnny or John Cody or
Elmore Purvis, or wonder who it was who had hit her
from behind that night. She just rode around with the
rest of the show, the ersatz Indians in full war regalia,
hats and bonnets and tomahawks and lots of whoop-
ing and hollering, and the Union soldiers, snappy in
their blue uniforms.

At one point she spotted Friar Malloy standing
among the crowd, looking on happily. She wondered
if she hadn't been wrong about him. Maybe he was
what he worked so hard to appear to be — a fat,
religious man who only meant to help.

The next time she came around, he was gone. Her
suspicions were instant, and a surprise to her because
she hadn't thought of it before.

What a perfect time to sneak back to the wagon
and look for the money.

He had not bathed in three days, and standing in the
chilled water of the creek seemed to cleanse not only
his body, but his soul as well.

He took his razor and a piece of soap he'd stuck in
his underwear and proceeded to shave himself right
there in the dying light of the afternoon.

You could hear the night birds now gathering in the
blooming branches of the trees, and the prairie dogs
hungry and barking as long shadows came.

If only he could free his mind and enjoy these things. . . .

He thought of Liz Archer, and again he could taste her on his lips. The recollection gave him an immediate, throbbing erection, but when he recalled further about his shame, his member went limp.

Already a vague plan was forming in his mind. He was going to ask Magda to go back East with him. There he could get on the vaudeville circuit, do his trick shooting routine, and not have to worry about the likes of Elmore Purvis.

Purvis . . .

The mere thought of the man made his scrotum shrivel. He would always carry that shame with him, no matter where he went or what he did.

It was crazy, anyway. Purvis blamed him for his brother's death, when all the time it had been the stupid kid's own fault.

But Purvis did not let the facts get in the way.

When his brother died in a shoot-out, he needed someone to blame.

And that, of course, was Billy Quick.

And what a stupid name that was! When he went back East, he was going to use his real name, Billy Quinn. Quick had been the captain's idea, and look at the trouble it had gotten him into.

Shaking his head, feeling the misery of the situation, he got out of the water, dried off, and headed back to camp.

He was headed for his wagon when he saw the considerable posterior of Friar Malloy sticking out of the back of Captain Barnaby's wagon.

Billy stopped, hid behind a tree, and watched.

Obviously, the monk assumed he was alone here in the camp. He moved without the slightest haste. As long as he could hear the music from the show, he would be safe.

Friar Malloy got down from the wagon and stood examining a scrap of paper he'd apparently taken from it.

Standing in the gentle dusk, the friar did a most un-friarlike thing. He took a pint of whiskey from beneath his robes and drained a good portion of it with one gulp.

"Shit," he said, shaking his head, looking around.

Billy continued to watch.

The friar put the pint back beneath his robes, then lifted his robes high and massaged his genitals roughly. After grunting a couple of times, he dropped the robe, crumpled the piece of paper in one big fist, and went over to the campfire to help himself to a cup of coffee.

By now Billy had aready formulated an idea of what was going on.

He drew his weapon and proceeded ahead to face the man who was calling himself Friar Malloy.

CHAPTER TWENTY-SIX

"That was the best show in my memory," Captain Barnaby announced afterward. "Thank you all."

The carnies obviously enjoyed his praise.

They broke into applause.

"Now go have yourselves a night."

They split into couples and small groups and headed into Weymouth, where the centennial ceremonies had begun.

Liz was brushing Blossom when Captain Barnaby strode over to her.

"You know what I haven't done today?" he asked.

His voice surprised her. She turned.

"I'm sorry, Captain. I guess I was lost in my own thoughts."

He repeated the question, obviously pleased with himself over something.

"No," she replied, "what haven't you done?"

"Haven't had a drink. Not one."

"That's wonderful."

"Do you know why?"

She shook her head.

"Because you inspired me."

"*I* inspired you?"

He nodded.

"How did I do that?"

"All the things you've been through in your young life, yet you're able to hold your head up high. You haven't given in to the temptations of liquor. You know, John Barleycorn can affect women as well as men."

"I know."

"So I figured, if you can be strong, with all your troubles, I can be strong with mine."

She smiled and said again, "That's wonderful, Captain. How do you feel?"

He put a hand straight out in front of him, and it was shaking.

"I'm scared as hell, to tell you the truth."

She slid her arm through his.

"You're going to do fine, and you're going to like yourself a whole hell of a lot more sober than drunk."

"I've already been sober enough to realize that my wife wouldn't have wanted me to be like this. She'd have wanted me to live life the way it should be lived."

Liz laughed.

"Captain, I wish I could inspire myself the way I seem to have inspired you."

"You remind me of her, you know," he said then, staring at her. "Of my wife, I mean."

"Do I?"

"She was blonde, like you, and almost as beautiful as you."

Given how the man still felt about his wife, Liz realized what a compliment that was.

Before the moment could get too awkward, Barnaby spoke again.

"I also wish you could inspire Billy Quick."

"Poor Billy and Magda."

"That Elmore Purvis! He's as much of a devil as they say he is."

"Maybe Billy will still get himself straightened out," she said, and then added to herself, after Elmore Purvis is dead.

The captain smiled wryly.

"Well, if I can give up demon rum for even a day, I suspect Billy can get rid of his demons, especially with Magda's help." He patted her on the shoulder and said, "How about I buy you dinner in town tonight?"

"That sounds like a good idea, Captain. A very good idea."

"Just who the hell are you?" Billy Quick demanded of the monk.

Friar Malloy put down his coffee cup.

"I am what you see, a man of God."

"Bullshit."

Friar Malloy shook his head.

"You are not a man of great faith."

"I saw you."

"You saw me?"

"I was watching you from behind a tree."

Friar Malloy seemed to consider Billy's words carefully. After a time he said, "You saw me take a drink, then?"

"You bet I did."

"Men of God are no more perfect than their fellow men —"

"You also said 'shit.' "

Friar Malloy, or whoever he was, startled Billy then by letting out a huge, bellowing laugh.

"If that is the worst word I ever utter in my life, my son, I will have lived a most exemplary life, I assure you."

Billy Quick wasn't about to be taken in by any smooth talk. He leveled his gun and said, "I'd like to see that piece of paper you stole from Captain Barnaby's wagon."

For the first time, Friar Malloy looked concerned.

This time Billy pushed the weapon right up to the monk's face.

"You've got ten seconds."

"You saw me, then?"

"I saw you." Billy put out his empty hand. "The paper, now."

"Ah, impetuous youth," Friar Malloy noted.

He placed the paper in Billy's hand.

It was too dark to read clearly, and if Billy concentrated too hard on it he'd have to take his eyes off the monk for too long.

"I can't read it."

"I'd say you have a problem, then."

"I'd say you have the problem if you don't tell me what it says."

Friar Malloy sighed.

"It doesn't say much, really."

"Let me be the judge of that."

"It says, 'Apply the seat of your pants to your riches.' "

Billy swore.

"Damn that Johnny and his riddles. He loved riddles."

The monk's eyes were intense now.

"Then it means nothing to you?"

Billy eyed him carefully.

"Just who in hell are you?"

"Maybe somebody who could make you rich."

"We're after the same thing, aren't we?"

"I'd say yes, we are."

Billy's eyes got very shrewd suddenly, and he said, "You're McCarthy, aren't you?"

"Why do you say that?"

"After he died, people started saying that Johnny was in cahoots with you. You're supposed to be a very bad man."

McCarthy laughed and said, " 'Judge not lest ye be judged.' "

"So you haven't found the money yet?"

"Does it look like it?"

Billy's grip tightened on his gun, and he said, "Do you know a man named Elmore Purvis?"

Apparently the answer was very important to the young man.

"I've heard of him."

"But you don't know him?"

"We've never met."

"You wouldn't try to lie to me, would you?"

"At this point?" McCarthy asked. "Don't be silly. We know all each other's secrets now, Mr. Billy Quick."

"I want that money."

"So do a lot of people, but maybe we have a better chance of getting it if we work together."

"Maybe. There are a couple of people here who have some of Billy's clues, but they haven't put them together yet. I can ask them some questions."

"They won't get suspicious?"

"Not if I ask right."

Billy found himself getting excited for the first time in three days. His cowardice in front of Elmore Purvis had left him dead inside. Now he was alive again. He would find the money, take his share, and he would have the grubstake he needed to get started back East. He would make Magda very happy.

"By tomorrow night, I'll have talked to the people here. You and I should meet."

"Where?"

"We'll be here for one more day. We'll meet in Weymouth, in the big saloon."

"What time?"

"After dark."

"Good. I'll be there."

Billy stared at him again.

"You sure you don't know a man called Purvis?"

The monk raised his hand as if about to swear on a Bible.

"I give you my word by all that is holy."

"Yeah," Billy Quick sneered, "I'll bet you do."

CHAPTER TWENTY-SEVEN

An hour later Purvis said, "Oh, that's beautiful, padre. That's a goddamned beautiful plan."

"Tomorrow night he tells us everything he knows and can find out about the money," McCarthy continued, "and then we kill him."

Purvis was still laughing.

"That stupid bastard didn't even suspect that we were partners?"

"He asked about it, but I convinced him that I didn't know you."

"I can't wait to see his face. He's mine, padre, all mine. Remember that."

"I remember."

Watching Purvis, McCarthy hoped he wasn't about to lose control right there in the saloon.

"I want to watch him turn pale as a sheet when he sees me. I want him to remember what my kid brother looked like lying dead in the street."

Purvis's eyes began to glitter, and spittle flew from his mouth.

"I want to see him shit his pants and wet himself just before I empty my gun into his face!"

Purvis wasn't laughing anymore. His vehemence was bordering on madness, and when he got like that the best thing to do was leave him alone.

McCarthy was glad he was not Billy Quick.

CHAPTER TWENTY-EIGHT

After midnight, Liz was awakened by a small hand shaking her shoulder.

"Come outside," Edgar whispered, and then was gone.

Liz rose and, carefully so as not to wake Evangeline and the others, left the wagon. Outside, the tiny form of Edgar waited impatiently for her, shifting his weight from one foot to the other.

"Higgins and I wondered if you'd want to talk to us."

"About what?"

The time she'd spent with Captain Barnaby in a Weymouth restaurant had relaxed her to some degree. She'd been able to fall into a deep sleep from which Edgar had now abruptly awakened her.

"The money."

"I'm real tired, Edgar. Couldn't this wait until morning?"

"We think we've figured something out," he said anxiously, "but we need somebody real smart to bounce it off."

She supposed she should have been flattered.

Liz rubbed her eyes and said, "All right. Just give me a few minutes to wake up."

"Meet us by that stand of pines over near the foothills."

"All right."

"One more thing, Edgar."

"What's that?"

"I want Captain Barnaby to be in on this too."

Edgar swore, and said, "You know how he is. He'll want to turn the money back to the bank where it came from."

"This might surprise you, Edgar."

"What?"

"So will I."

Elmore Purvis walked down the street. Grinning. Hands on his gun. A crowd had gathered to watch.

"You ready?" Purvis called to Billy Quick, who stood twenty yards away.

Billy tried to answer, but he had no voice.

"I asked you if you were ready," Purvis called again loudly. He looked at the crowd and they laughed with him, as if on cue.

"This time you ain't got no choice, Quick," Purvis said. "I'm firing whether you draw or not."

Billy's hands dropped to his guns.

His fancy, useless guns.

Just as he had no voice, he seemed to have no coordination.

His hands trembled.

Shook.

Uselessly.

"Well, I don't know about you folks, but I've had about enough of this."

The crowd laughed with him again.

And Purvis went for his guns. . . .

Billy woke, soaked in sweat.

Nearby, a lone coyote called out in the night.

Nearer, Magda snored softly, her face beautiful and fragile and peaceful. Billy envied her that peace.

His head sank into his hands.

Coward!

That's what he was, and there was no way of getting around it.

Not even in his dreams had he been able to defeat Elmore Purvis.

Then he heard voices.

At first he thought they might be fragments of his dream still playing in his mind, but then he recognized Captain Barnaby's voice.

Thinking of the captain brought back the conversation he'd had earlier with the phony monk, McCarthy.

He eased up from his cot and put his head cautiously outside the wagon. He saw Captain Barnaby and Liz Archer talking, walking away from camp. The captain was carrying a lantern.

Billy decided that this was worth investigating. He dressed quickly and stepped out into the night.

CHAPTER TWENTY-NINE

Captain Barnaby carried a lantern to guide Liz and himself to their rendezvous with Edgar and Tony Higgins.

Thick ground fog made passage hazardous. A sprained ankle from a fall could be mighty troublesome.

Liz said, "Do you really think they have some notion about where the money is?"

Captain Barnaby nodded.

"They just might. Or at least they may have enough of a notion for us all to sit together and figure it all out."

Liz frowned.

"If Johnny Shilstone is watching now, I suppose he must be pretty amused at all of us running around in circles, trying to figure out where the money is."

"That would be Johnny, all right. He loved confounding people."

Suddenly Tony Higgins appeared from nowhere.

"There's a shallow cave just ahead. Let's go in there."

He led the way.

Edgar had a small fire going in the cave. Flames played off the ribbed clay walls. Animal bones of various kinds shone whitely in the firelight.

Liz and Captain Barnaby sat on one log, Edgar and Tony Higgins on a facing one. The fire was between them.

"I guess you should start, Tony," she said, rubbing her eyes.

Higgins nodded.

"Earlier tonight, Edgar and I were talking about some things Johnny said over the past few weeks."

Edgar eagerly agreed.

"What got us thinking was the 'red wagon' phrase he wrote down for you."

The captain shrugged.

"I'd almost written that off as so much delirium."

"Yeah, but think of what Johnny said to Black Feather awhile back. 'Where the red wagon sits.' "

Liz frowned again.

"I'm afraid that doesn't make things any clearer. At least, not for me."

Captain Barnaby agreed.

"We don't have a red wagon in this show."

"Ah," Tony Higgins said, obviously enjoying his role center stage, "but we did."

"We did?" the captain asked, puzzled. "When?"

"About ten years ago, Captain, when I first joined the show."

"I don't remember it," Captain Barnaby maintained stubbornly.

"Sure, Captain. It was the one that female sharp-shooter used to ride in."

Captain Barnaby rubbed his forehead vigorously, obviously trying to bring back his faulty memory.

Too many years of drinking, he was thinking.

"Damn . . ."

Then he snapped his fingers.

"Wait a minute. Sure! The red wagon with the faded painting of Annie Oakley on the side."

"That's the one," Edgar said.

Now Captain Barnaby was really puzzled.

"But that wagon is long gone."

For the first time Tony showed disappointment.

"Are you sure about that?"

"Yes, why?"

"You don't think that maybe we just painted it over and used it for something else?"

"No," Captain Barnaby said. "It's coming back to me now. About five years ago we traded in most of the wagons, remember? They were falling apart."

Edgar jumped down off the log. The firelight made his shadow on the wall behind him far larger than his body would ever be. It loomed over him as he paced back and forth in front of the others. He reminded Liz of a story she had heard as a small child.

What was it called?

Oh, yes . . .

Rumpelstiltskin.

"Think hard, Captain," Edgar said. "There's a lot at stake here."

Captain Barnaby shrugged again.

"I'm sure we traded it in. Positive."

"Damn," said Tony Higgins. "I had plans for

what I was going to do with that money too."

"Let's get something straight right now," Captain Barnaby said. "If we find that money, it goes back to the bank."

"What?" Higgins said. "What happened to finders keepers?"

"It doesn't apply here."

Higgins looked at Liz, who said, "I feel the same way, Tony."

"But —"

"Look," Liz said, interrupting him, "there might be a reward, and that's all yours and Edgar's. How's that?"

Not completely satisfied, Higgins said, "I guess that'll have to do."

"Now let's think about this," Liz said. "There's one way to tell for sure if that wagon is gone."

"How?" Captain Barnaby asked.

"We'll have to take a knife, or something sharp, and scrape the paint off of all the wagons. If there's one that's red underneath, it's probably the one we're looking for — and it doesn't even have to be the one you're all talking about."

"But say we find a red wagon," Captain Barnaby said. "What does that prove?"

" 'Where the red wagon sits,' " Higgins quoted. "It's got to mean something. When we find a red wagon, we'll tear it apart if we have to."

"I think I've got an idea," Edgar said.

They all turned their attention to him.

"What if it's just a, whatayacallit, a play on words?"

"What is?" Higgins asked.

" 'Where the red wagon sits,' " Edgar said. "What if Johnny meant that the money is in the red wagon, where you sit?"

They all thought about it, and Captain Barnaby said, "Maybe . . ."

"Sure, what else could it mean?"

"The first thing we have to do is check all the wagons," Liz said. "Take a knife to the paint and see if you can find any red under it."

"That sounds like the best idea," Captain Barnaby said.

"Well, let's go. . . ." Edgar said.

"I think we'd better wait until morning," Liz said. "I don't think it would be wise to wake everyone up in the middle of the night. We don't want a mini-gold rush on our hands."

"Oh, come on," Edgar said. "Morning? Let's do it now —"

"You heard Liz," Captain Barnaby said. "I don't think we should wake everyone up. In the morning they'll all be in town for breakfast or shopping."

"It makes sense, Edgar," Higgins said.

"Bah!" Edgar said, but he bowed to the will of the majority.

"One more thing," Captain Barnaby said.

"What now?" Edgar said.

"I think the town marshal should be in on this."

"The marshal?" Higgins asked. "You may want to think that over, Captain."

"Nothing to think about."

"You're sure about that?"

"I'm very sure." The captain stood up and walked to the mouth of the cave. "Come on, let's get back to camp."

Liz rose first and followed him, and as Tony Higgins stood up Edgar put his little hand on the man's arm to get his attention.

"I think I liked him better drunk. . . ."

Billy Quick had been standing next to the cave's entrance and listened to every word.

His heart beat wildly now as he ran on ahead back to camp, almost falling headlong more than once.

He had already made up his mind about one thing. He wanted no partners in this venture. He wanted the money for himself and Magda. By the time tomorrow night rolled around and McCarthy came looking for him, he, Magda, and the money would be long gone.

He crept into his cot, trying not to wake Magda, but without success.

"Billy, what is it?" she asked, peering over at him through the gloom of her wagon.

"Nothing."

"Are you all right?"

"I'm fine."

"You're soaked with perspiration." She raised herself up onto one elbow in order to take a better look at him. "Did you go out?"

"Just outside the wagon for a moment," he said. "I had a bad dream and wanted to get some air."

She reached to touch him tenderly and asked, "Do you want to tell me about it?"

"Tomorrow," he said, kissing her. "Tomorrow I'll tell you all about it. Just go back to sleep now, and remember I love you."

"I love you too," she said, obviously pleased — and somewhat mollified — by the words.

As she quickly fell back to sleep, he remained

awake, staring at nothing. In his mind he was already spending the money. He could see himself and Magda in a fancy New York restaurant. He could see them with the best of everything. His memories of Elmore Purvis and his own shame would be virtually gone and forgotten. He would never have to tolerate anyone's insults again.

In the morning all his dreams and wishes would come true.

He would wait for the others to find the red wagon and the money, and then take it from them.

Even if it meant killing someone.

CHAPTER THIRTY

"So, Billy Quick is going to help us find the money. Isn't that nice of him?"

McCarthy's hands were greasy from his breakfast of ham hocks and biscuits, and he wiped them on his monk's robes.

"Very nice of him."

Purvis was still gloating, as he had been doing last night, and McCarthy was doing the simplest thing by agreeing with him.

"And you're supposed to meet him tonight?"

McCarthy nodded.

"At the saloon."

"You gonna dress like that when you meet him?"

"After sundown tonight, I'm through with this disguise, Purvis," McCarthy said, fingering the beads around his waist. "I only need it for one more errand this afternoon."

"What errand would that be?"

"I'm going to make friends with a certain young lady."

"The blonde? I don't blame you."

"No, not the blonde. This woman's name is Evangeline Hart. I saw her in the show yesterday." McCarthy's eyes became glassy with undisguised lust, and he smiled. "She reminds me of a girl I knew in Boston."

Now it was Purvis's turn to smile.

"You're getting sentimental, McCarthy. I never thought I'd see that in you. You must have cared a lot for this woman in Boston."

"I did," McCarthy said. "That's precisely why I cut her throat."

By ten that morning Evangeline Hart was hard at work doing what she'd promised herself she'd do for the past two months — clean up her wagon. Back home in Ohio she'd been considered — despite her lovely brunette looks and charming manner — the least of three sisters because she did not take care of the domestic chores. Her parents had not been entirely unhappy to see her leave.

Now, sweeping out her wagon, she noticed a bluebird sitting on the branch of a nearby elm.

She watched the creature for the next few minutes, listening intently to its song, observing how it perched so precariously on its narrow perch.

Then Evangeline's eyes dropped to the scene just below the branch.

Liz Archer, the beautiful blonde woman with whom she shared a wagon, stood talking quietly with Captain Barnaby, Edgar, and Tony Higgins.

Evangeline felt only a small pang of regret at being excluded. As the pretty girl who always played the virgin about to be despoiled by a variety of villains, she found herself considered too young and unsophisticated to be included in most conversations. She was, to men and women alike, little more than an attractive prop.

The funny thing was, she felt a certain amount of pain now only because Liz Archer had been so nice to her since she had joined their caravan. Over several meals, Liz had listened with real interest to Evangeline's conversation, and the younger woman had responded with a virtual flood of opinions on everything from the Congress of the United States to the growing debate over the gold standard.

She'd been so much a part of Liz's conversations that she almost resented the fact that she was not being included in the one that was going on now.

She wondered what they were talking about so intently. . . .

"Looks like most of the people have gone into town," Captain Barnaby said. "This will probably be the best time to do it."

"What about Evangeline?" Liz asked. "I saw her earlier. She may still be around."

"Don't worry about her," Edgar said. "She's too dumb to notice anything."

Liz flushed at that.

"She's a very bright young woman, Edgar, as you'd find out if you took the time to sit and talk to her for a little while."

"What I want from Vangy is not talk," Edgar said with a leer.

"Evangeline, bright?" Tony Higgins asked. He shook his head and said, "I'm afraid I'd have to agree with Edgar on that one, Liz. She's pretty enough, all right, but God surely didn't grace her with a lot of brains."

"Well, you're both wrong, but we don't have time to argue over it now." She took a bowie knife from her belt, brandished it, and said, "Are we ready, then?"

Captain Barnaby nodded.

"We'll each take five wagons," he instructed. "If anybody finds anything, don't yell out, just come quietly and find the rest of us."

"Fine," Liz agreed, and Edgar and Tony nodded.

"All right, then. Let's go."

Having finished cleaning her wagon, Evangeline decided to complete her housecleaning by taking some dirty clothes to the creek for washing. On the way she passed Liz, who was kneeling down by one of the wagons.

"I'm going down to the creek, Liz. Care to join me?" she asked.

"No, thanks," Liz said, looking up from whatever it was she was doing. "I told the captain I'd help him with something."

"Well," Evangeline said when Liz didn't offer to explain any further, "suit yourself, but if you change your mind I'll be down there for a while."

Liz smiled.

"Have a nice time."

"Are you not ashamed?" Magda asked.

Billy Quick, who was seated across from her in a Weymouth restaurant, said nothing.

He had assumed that once he told Magda of his plans and she realized how close they were to getting the money for themselves, she would be delighted to go along with it.

Instead, she was angry.

"You didn't answer my question, Billy."

"No, I'm not ashamed."

"Then you should be."

"I'm doing what's necessary for us."

"Don't say that. You are talking about betraying our friends. Don't say that the reason is us."

Billy was hardly listening. He was wondering how they were doing back at camp. Had they found the money yet? He hoped not. His plan had been to accompany Magda to town so they'd think he was gone, and then double back. He was anxious to get going, but Magda wanted to argue.

"Billy, listen to me," she said. "We are talking about our friends here. Just think of what these people have done for you. They have stood by you, and this is how you would repay them? I can't believe this of you, Billy. I just can't."

"You know what I am, Magda."

"I know what you are afraid you are."

He slammed his fist on the table, attracting the attention of nearby diners.

"It's what I am, and nothing can change that."

Abruptly, he stood up and said, "I have to go, Magda. Don't come back to camp for a while."

"Billy, please . . ." she called out, but he was already gone.

It was hot, stifling hot inside the monk's robes.

McCarthy stood behind a copse of lodgepole pines and watched Evangeline Hart wash her clothes in the creek.

The scene reminded McCarthy of a painting. The sky was the blue of schooner days. On the other side of the creek, two small kittens rolled and tumbled in play. In the sparkling water itself, just downstream from the woman, fish snapped up into the air.

Evangeline completed the picture.

She was wearing a simple skirt and a peasant blouse, and she had gotten so wet that the blouse clung to her, outlining perfectly rounded, small breasts, the nipples clearly outlined against the damp fabric.

McCarthy kneaded his erection through the robes.

He was going to start out being nice to her and see if that worked. Maybe she would willingly give him what he wanted. However, if she repulsed him, as that woman in Boston had done, well, he'd get what he wanted anyway.

Liz worked on her third wagon.

With equipment this old, getting to the bare wood took some doing. The painters, who had lavished layer after layer of coating on the wagons to make the gaudy illustrations last as long as possible through rain and snow, had made finding the base color virtually impossible.

Liz's wrist was already getting stiff from all the scraping, but she persisted. The money was going to be her snare to lure Elmore Purvis. Thought of that kept her working on.

At one point Edgar's voice blurted out excitedly —

exactly what Captain Barnaby had told them not to do — and the little man came running over, excitement giving his features a childlike aspect.

"You'd better come and look," he said. "I think I found it."

Liz and Edgar rounded up Captain Barnaby and Tony Higgins and went to check it out.

When they got there, Edgar proudly showed them the side of a wagon that depicted a fearsome cavalry-Indian battle. He had scraped sections of the rear down through several coats.

Faded red paint showed through.

Liz did not get as excited as Edgar. Quickly, she took her knife and went to work on the red paint. At first the stuff did not change colors, but then gradually traces of white began to show through the streaks of red.

There was a coat beneath.

This had not originally been a red wagon.

"Damn," Tony Higgins said.

When she turned to look at Edgar, she saw that the little man had silver tears of frustration in his eyes.

She thought she knew how he felt.

"Let's get back to work," she said.

They started scraping again.

Purvis sat near a window in one of Weymouth's saloons.

When he saw Billy Quick hurrying past, he came out of his chair quickly, startling three nearby drinkers.

He had been wanting to kill Billy Quick for a long time, and here was a perfect opportunity.

Then reason overtook him and he sat down.

Quick had to be alive to meet with McCarthy that night. When that meeting was over, Purvis would have all that he wanted. Billy Quick's death, and the money from the bank robbery.

He thought about McCarthy now, who had gone out to camp after that little gal. McCarthy's appetites bothered Purvis. It was one thing to kill, and another to take perverse pleasure in it. He hoped that McCarthy's plans for the girl wouldn't ruin any of their plans.

Suddenly he slammed his beer mug on the table and stood up. He was going to go out there to make sure that nothing happened that would cost them the money.

CHAPTER THIRTY-ONE

"Good afternoon, friar," Evangeline Hart said, watching the huge religious man emerge from the woods.

"Good afternoon, my child," McCarthy said. With a broad sweep of his hand, he indicated the day. "God has smiled on us today, has He not?"

She nodded her agreement.

"He most certainly has, friar."

He came closer.

And put out his hand.

"I am Friar Malloy."

"I know. I saw you around camp."

"I saw you as well, yesterday when you performed. You are a very good actress. God has blessed you."

"That's very kind of you to say."

He eyed the pile of freshly washed clothes that she had piled on a nearby rock and added, "And a clean one, I see."

Suddenly Evangeline became very uncomfortable and aware of what she was wearing. The friar seemed to be watching her breasts a little too intently.

She bent over to pick up the clothes basket and her breasts moved, causing McCarthy's mouth to become dry.

"Well, friar, it was nice to see you."

"And to have seen you, my child. Have a good day."

Suddenly he was gone, moving much more quickly than a man of his bulk should have been able to. She found herself relieved to see him go.

As she started back for camp, she could not get the image of his gaze out of her mind. She had seen that look before on the faces of men, but never on the face of a man of God. Then again, priests and friars, weren't they still just men? Perhaps she was over-reacting.

She had just entered the densest part of the forest when suddenly Friar Malloy was there again. He grabbed her, causing her to drop her clean clothes into the dirt, and put one hand over her mouth and the other around her waist, lifting her off the ground.

She did not even have time to scream.

The fourth wagon Liz worked on yielded an under-coating of red paint.

For a few seconds she felt her heart begin to beat faster. Remembering what had happened with Edgar, she kept quiet and continued to scrape. Eventually, she saw unmistakable traces of yellow beneath the red.

Drained, she sank down on a nearby rock and

wondered if Johnny Shilstone had been having pointless fun with his friends. But the note he had written in the captain's wagon, while in great pain, that certainly could not have been for fun.

She was about to get up to start on her fifth wagon when Captain Barnaby came walking over to her.

"I found it."

Elmore Purvis stood on a ridge just above the camp where the Wild West show wagons were pulled into a wide semicircle and watched the commotion below.

He had found no trace of McCarthy, which worried him a great deal. That worry dissipated, however, in the face of what was going on in camp.

Purvis had a hunch that they might have found the money, and hunkered down to watch patiently. As soon as he knew for sure, he'd take a walk down into camp and make his presence known.

For now, he just watched.

Billy Quick bounced around the cold and angry form of Magda like a small puppy seeking favors. She had followed him from the restaurant and upon catching up to him, refused to speak to him.

"I'm doing this for us."

"If you say that again I will scream," she said, breaking the silence. "You are doing this because you are a selfish person."

With that, she quickened her pace, getting ahead of him, and he stopped, watching her continue on with quick, angry steps. Then he thought again of the fresh start the money would give them and hurried to catch up to her.

Magda would come around to his way of thinking. He knew she would.

"This is the wagon, all right," Liz said.

They had taken turns trying to get past the coat of red paint. Below it was only primer, and then bare wood.

This was indeed the right wagon.

"Now we've got to figure out what Johnny meant by 'where it sits,' " Edgar said.

"Damn Johnny and his word games," Tony Higgins said.

"Remember what Edgar said last night?" Liz asked. "Let's try that."

With that, the four of them moved to the front of the wagon and began examining the seat.

A minute later Tony Higgins, excited, said, "Look at this!"

He hadn't meant to break her neck.

McCarthy stood sweating profusely inside his scratching monk's robes, looking down at the naked and bloody form of Evangeline Hart.

He had stripped her easily enough, like peeling a piece of fruit, and then slapped her several times to keep her quiet. He'd straddled her, hiked up his monk's robes to expose his erection, and as he was about to enter her had grabbed her by the back of the neck . . . and it snapped! Just like a piece of dry wood!

He stood there now, his erection huge and pulsing. He eyed the dead woman now with a certain curiosity.

How would it be, he wondered? After all, she *was* still warm.

Or maybe, he thought, feeling his cock through the robes, he should just take care of it himself.

And then, through the thickness of the trees, he saw a flash of white.

A blouse, he was sure of it. A woman's white blouse.

He ran through the tangled underbrush and peered through a clump of trees.

A beautiful dark-haired woman stalked through the forest, and he recognized her as the gypsy woman from the show.

Not far behind her trotted that fool, Billy Quick.

He watched as Billy Quick called out to her and she stopped abruptly. Apparently they had been arguing and the man was trying to make amends.

McCarthy, almost blinded by his need for a woman, eyed her large breasts anxiously. Drawing his knife, he left the underbrush and worked his way around behind them. With one expert flick of his wrist, he sent the knife flying through the air. It landed with a dull smack and embedded itself in Billy Quick's back, high up near the left shoulder blade.

Before Magda could realize what had happened and scream, McCarthy was upon her.

The top of the seat could be raised on creaky, rusted hinges. Inside was a false box that gave way to yet another hinged lid.

Captain Barnaby looked inside, and his heart sank.

"It's empty."

"It can't be," Edgar complained.

The midget scrambled up onto the seat and stuck his head inside, then his shoulder. Comically, he almost disappeared from view inside the box.

Captain Barnaby looked at Liz, who shrugged.

Tony Higgins said, "Damn that Johnny."

Billy wondered if this was one of his nightmares.

He was lying on the ground on his stomach with a searing pain in his back, watching as, in what appeared to be slow motion, McCarthy slapped Magda down to the ground, tore off her clothes, then relieved himself of his monk's robes and proceeded to brutally rape her.

And Billy couldn't move.

CHAPTER THIRTY-TWO

Liz was the one who noticed a cleft in the wagon.

She, Captain Barnaby, Edgar, and Tony Higgins were all standing glumly around the seat that had proved to be empty, wondering what to do next, when Liz noticed what looked like a peculiar configuration down the center of the wagon.

She walked away from the others and inspected the wagon close up.

It appeared as if the wagon had at one time been sawed in half and then nailed back together.

Then she realized what most likely had happened.

What if both parts of the wagon were front parts?

What if — if that were the case — both contained front seats?

Then that would mean . . .

Liz went to work quickly. . . .

Purvis had eventually worked his way down to the level of the camp and was now watching from behind some trees.

They had initially appeared to be very excited about something, but now suddenly they were downcast.

Elmore Purvis was getting frustrated.

He wanted his money.

Magda had never felt such pain.

Not only had she been raped viciously, as if the man had been trying to split her apart with his huge erection — but the friar — the friar! — had beaten her severely, both punching her before the rape and kicking her afterward.

Blood ran thickly from her nose and mouth as she rose up onto her elbow. She peered around and found the friar watching her.

"So," he sneered at her. "You're ready for seconds already, eh? You gypsy women really love it, huh?"

In a single stride he went over to her and kicked her in the ribs.

Magda cried out and fell back, closing her eyes, saying a silent prayer that she would die before he could have her again. . . .

Elmore Purvis edged out from behind the trees.

The sudden way the four people had converged at the other end of the wagon convinced him that they had found something.

At last!

Liz could not help smiling.

Just as she'd suspected, when the wagon had been put together from parts of two different ones, the fronts of both wagons had been used.

What was now the back section also contained a front seat, complete with hinged seat.

Now the others crowded around her in response to her call.

"Hurry up," Edgar said, dancing about on his small legs.

"Yes," Captain Barnaby said, his eagerness less uncontained, but no less intense, "hurry."

When he came back to consciousness this time, Billy Quick saw that the rape of Magda was still going on — or was happening again.

Now he knew it was no nightmare.

He also knew that he had to help Magda or she would be dead soon.

He tried to get up, and the pain in his back radiated in wider and wider circles. He still had no idea what was causing it. Had he been shot in the back?

He tried again to get up, but the pain was too much.

Amid Magda's cries of pain, muffled by McCarthy, he fell unconscious again.

The back seat was very much like the front one. Inside were two hinged compartments, almost like Chinese boxes, and finally there was a lid leading to a third compartment.

It was secured with a fat padlock.

Liz knew that trying to shoot the lock apart would most likely be futile and could well be dangerous. At such close quarters a bullet could easily ricochet, injuring or even killing the person doing the shooting.

She turned around to Tony Higgins, who was almost as muscular as a circus strongman.

"Do you have a crowbar and a hammer?"

"Sure. Why?"

"Go and get them. And hurry."

"You bet."

He came back inside of three minutes.

With Edgar and Captain Barnaby hovering nearby, Liz and the fire-eater went to work.

Purvis decided that this was as good a time as any for a closer look.

He left the shelter of the trees and edged along the grass to where the wagons were circled.

He got up close enough to hear the midget say, "This is it. I can feel it in my bones. As soon as they get that padlock open, we'll all be rich. You wait and see."

Purvis smiled.

He had every reason to be just as happy as the midget was.

Within the next few minutes, all the money was going to be his.

CHAPTER THIRTY-THREE

Billy Quick struggled to his feet.

McCarthy had just rolled away from Magda and was reaching for his trousers when Billy staggered over to him.

With strength he didn't think he possessed, Billy raised his foot and kicked McCarthy hard in the side of the head. McCarthy, however, surprised that Billy was still alive, shook off the meager kick. He drew his bowie knife from the sheath around his middle. It was still stained with Billy's blood, as McCarthy had not cleaned it when he pulled it free of Billy's back.

He got to his feet and said, "I'm going to enjoy this, Billy boy. Too bad I can't save you for Purvis, but I'm going to enjoy this too much to give it up."

It was obvious that he meant to finish the job he had started earlier.

Billy, still very shaky, looked around frantically for

a place to escape McCarthy's knife. He moved to his left and bumped into a tree. He moved to his right and very nearly tripped over Magda.

"First, though, you're going to tell me where the money is."

"I don't know," Billy gasped. It still felt as if a red-hot poker were sticking in his back.

McCarthy lunged with the knife and slashed Billy's right arm, which bled profusely. Billy, already weakened, fell to his knees. Through shimmering vision he saw McCarthy coming at him.

McCarthy grabbed Billy by the hair and said, "Where's the money?"

"Don't know."

McCarthy drew the knife straight across Billy's forehead. It was a shallow cut, but head wounds bleed profusely and this one was no exception.

With his own blood clouding his vision, Billy wished for death for the first time in his life.

The lock took five minutes to open.

By the time they finished, Tony Higgins was covered with sweat and breathing heavily.

"Now," he said to Liz, "look inside and see if the money's there."

She paused for a moment, recalling all the bad things that had happened in pursuit of this money. Maybe the best thing to do would be to toss a match in there and burn it.

If it was there.

"C'mon," Edgar said impatiently, "hurry!"

"I want you all to know that my intentions are to return this money to its rightful owners."

"Aw, shit!" Edgar said.

"That's what I told them," Captain Barnaby said.

"Nobody would know if we took it," Tony Higgins said.

"Sure," Edgar said, "it would be our little secret."

"You know better than that," Liz told Edgar and Tony.

Unwilling to give in, Tony Higgins tried an entirely new tack.

"What if we said we only found half of it and kept only half?"

"Or even a fourth."

Liz laughed at them.

"I wish you two could see yourselves, see what money has turned you into."

Edgar scowled.

"I haven't had an easy life, being a midget and all. That money couldn't turn me into anything worse than what I already am."

"I didn't know you felt that way," Tony Higgins said, suddenly more concerned about Edgar than about the money.

"There's lots of things about me you don't know."

"Well, maybe you just need a good friend," Tony said, draping a big arm over the midget's small shoulders. "Go ahead, Liz, take a look inside there and see what you find."

Liz looked inside.

The moment he saw the big, white canvas bag being removed from the seat, Purvis made his move.

He came around the corner of a nearby wagon and, gun drawn, said, "I believe that's mine."

"Have you ever watched somebody get their throat cut?" McCarthy asked Billy.

By now Billy was suffering from four additional cuts, each bleeding profusely. These wounds, plus the deeper one in his back, were slowly draining the life out of him.

"Maybe," McCarthy said, hunkering down in front of Billy so the sharpshooter could see him clearly, "maybe I'll cut your girlfriend's tits off and then cut her throat right in front of you before I cut yours."

McCarthy laughed, and he was so intent on laughing that he didn't see what Billy saw behind the man through pain-clouded eyes.

Incredibly, though she was battered and bleeding, Magda had picked herself up from the ground. She found a large tree branch on the ground and advanced on McCarthy from behind, somehow summoning the strength to hold it up over her head.

"Or maybe," McCarthy said, putting the point of the knife right under Billy Quick's chin, "I'll just get it over with for you."

Once again McCarthy grabbed Billy by the hair, and brutally bending his head back, he prepared to slit his exposed throat.

Magda brought the chunk of wood up with both hands and brought it crashing down on McCarthy's head.

"Run!" she cried to Billy, helping him up. "Oh, God, Billy, let's run!"

CHAPTER THIRTY-FOUR

Liz handed the money over to Purvis reluctantly.

"I'll find you, Purvis, wherever you go."

"Not me, honey," he said. "You don't want me, you want the man who shot you and your horse."

"And that wasn't you?"

"If it was, you'd both be dead, wouldn't you?"

He had a point there. A man like Elmore Purvis would not have missed.

"What are you saying?"

"McCarthy's the one you want. He's the one who bushwhacked you. I only bought into this game when I found out how much money he was after. I wasn't even part or the original robbery, but I've got the money now, haven't I?"

"Yes, you have."

Purvis was about to say something else when Magda came screaming into the camp, dragging a very bloody Billy Quick with her.

"The monk raped me! He tried to kill us!" Magda shouted.

She and Billy Quick saw Purvis at the same time.

"Oh, God!" Magda said, stopping in her tracks. Billy literally hung at her side, his arm over her shoulder. Liz would not have thought that Magda had that much strength.

At that point, McCarthy showed up in camp. He was brandishing his bowie knife, and his eyes glittered with madness.

Purvis, realizing that the situation could get out of hand and possibly cost him what he had, made a decision and carried it out in a split second.

"This time I'm gonna cut your balls off," McCarthy said, waving the bloody knife.

Purvis had the impression that McCarthy didn't even know where he was. All he knew was his blood lust.

As McCarthy started for Billy and Magda, Liz wondered if she could draw and kill him before Purvis killed her.

She didn't have to.

Purvis turned and carried out his decision, firing one shot that took McCarthy right through the heart. The man stopped cold, as if he had run into a brick wall. From his eyes Purvis could see that he knew what had happened to him, but couldn't believe it.

"That's the breaks," he said to McCarthy, but the other man was past hearing or caring.

He was dead.

"Why did you do that?" Liz asked.

"I got tired of him and his sick games. All I ever wanted since I joined up with him was the money."

"Then you weren't part of the original bank robbery gang?"

Purvis grinned and said, "After their last job, McCarthy took care of all of them except Shilstone. He was the one who knew where the money was."

"And now you've got it, but there's one other thing you've got to do."

"What's that?"

She reached inside her collar and pulled out the orange bandanna.

"You've got to kill me, or word will get around that you backed down from me."

"You're crazy."

"When that happens, every punk with a gun will come looking for you. Your life will be an even worse hell than I know it is now."

"What are you suggesting?"

"Holster your gun and let's see who's the best, Purvis — if you're not afraid."

"You against me, huh?"

"Right."

"And you think I don't know who you are?" Purvis sneered. "I thought I recognized that bandanna the first time I saw you, Miss Angel Eyes, but I figured I had to be wrong."

"Why?"

"Because you don't exist."

"I don't?"

He shook his head.

"There isn't a woman alive who can outshoot a man."

"That's what we're here to find out, Purvis — and even after you kill me, you'll still have to kill all of the others," she said, sweeping her arm to indicate the rest of the people in the camp.

"Believe me," he said, "that's no problem."

"*They're* no problem, you mean. On the other hand, I am."

"What problem are you?"

"I can take you."

"Never, lady."

"Then put your gun up and we'll see."

Captain Barnaby said, "Liz," but she ignored him. She also ignored the flashback she was having of John Cody, gun already drawn, still being beaten by Elmore Purvis.

"What do you say, Elmore? Are you going to back down from a woman just because she wears an orange bandanna?"

"I've never backed down from anyone," he said, dropping the money sack to the ground, "least of all a woman." He holstered his gun and said, "I want you to know one thing, though."

"What?"

"I'm too smart for this ploy of yours, but I'm going for it anyway, because I can take you."

"Not on your best day, Elmore."

Purvis smiled and said, "You'll be my first woman."

"And your last. . . ."

Purvis drew, and in that split second between life and death, he knew that he had made the wrong decision.

CHAPTER THIRTY-FIVE

Two weeks later the Wild West show pulled into a meadow outside the town of Coulton, Nevada. It would be their last stop in Nevada — and it would be Liz Archer's last stop with them altogether.

After what had happened in Weymouth, Liz had decided to stay with Captain Barnaby's show until Billy Quick was well enough to handle his gun. He wore his arm in a sling most of the time, but for the most recent show he had removed it and left it hanging down at his left side while he fired with his right hand, his aim unerring.

Though many things had been resolved — the threats of Elmore Purvis and Ernest McCarthy, the whereabouts of the money, who had shot Liz and Blossom — there were still others that were not yet resolved.

One of those was Billy Quick's self-esteem, but Liz

doubted that she could help him with that. It was going to be up to him to do something about it, with Magda's support.

Secondly came the money and what to do with it. Barnaby and Liz decided that when they reached Coulton they would telegraph the proper authorities and hold the money until they were told what to do with it. Edgar and Tony Higgins complained halfheartedly, but both were looking forward to whatever reward would be offered.

Last, Liz still had not found the men who had robbed her and caused Blossom's initial injury — and, in a sense, started this whole chain of events, for had Liz been riding Blossom instead of walking her, she might never have found Johnny Shilstone tied to that tree.

Now Liz felt she had traveled with the show long enough. It was time to go out on her own once more, astride a healthy Blossom, and hopefully find the six men who had robbed her.

When camp was made, Barnaby went looking for Liz and found her talking to Magda.

"I'm going into town to send the telegraph message to the authorities. Care to come along?"

"Sure, Captain," Liz said. "Magda?"

"I will wait here for Billy to come back," Magda said. Her eyes were sad, and the captain noticed.

"What's wrong with her?" he asked as they started for town.

"Billy left early this morning. She's afraid he went into town to drink."

"I don't know if that boy is going to straighten out or not," Captain Barnaby said with a worried frown.

"We can't all have the courage of a lion, you know."

"I know," Liz said, nodding, "but apparently Billy Quick doesn't."

"And nobody can tell him. . . ."

When they hit town, they went to the telegraph office and sent the telegram.

"Where are you headed now?" she asked him as they stepped outside.

"I've got some posters with me. I think I'll hang them up around town. What about you?"

"I'm thirsty from the walk. I think I'll go over to the saloon."

Immediately, she cursed herself for a fool. Captain Barnaby licked his lips as she said "saloon," and she remembered that once again he was trying to give up what he called "demon rum."

"I'm sorry. . . ."

"That's all right. You go ahead. It'll take me some time to get rid of all these posters. I'll meet you back here in a couple of hours, and we'll see if we've got an answer."

"All right."

They split up and Liz went to the Coulton House Saloon, which was connected to the Coulton House Hotel.

Inside she approached the bar and ordered a beer. She was conscious of the looks she was getting, but chose to ignore them. Crouched over her beer, she looked in the mirror and saw Billy Quick seated at a rear table. She picked up her beer and strode across the room to where he was sitting.

"Hello, Billy."

He had a half-full bottle of liquor in front of him and looked up from his drink at her. .

"Hello, Liz," he said. "Care to join me — if you're not too embarrassed to be seen with me."

"Don't be silly, Billy," she said, sitting down and setting her beer on the table. "You know Magda's worried about you, don't you?"

"She shouldn't be. She should go on living her own life, Liz. We can't ever have a life together. Not after what I've done."

"And what have you done?"

"I was willing to rob my friends to get the money I wanted. What kind of man does that? What kind of man can't protect his woman from another man?"

He was still despondent over the fact that Magda had been raped and he hadn't been able to help her. Instead, it had been she who had gotten up off the ground and saved *his* life.

"I think you're letting your male ego get in the way here, Billy."

"My ego? What ego?"

"You can't accept the fact that Magda saved your life instead of you saving hers."

"She'd have done us all a favor if she had let McCarthy kill me."

She didn't know what to say to that. She couldn't think of anything to say to him that would make a difference.

"I'm sorry, Billy," she said, picking up her beer and standing up. "Sorry for you. I can't try to help you anymore."

"I'm beyond help."

"Yes," she said sadly, "I can see that now."

She took her beer and started back across the room

toward the bar. On the way she passed a table where five men were playing poker. Something caught her eye and she stopped, frowning. What was it? . . . And then there it was!

One of the players wore something around his neck, looped through a length of leather. It was a flattened piece of metal with an ace of spades stamped onto it.

It was the ace of spades given to her by Chance Taker, the one that had been taken from her neck by one of the six men who had robbed her.

She waited now, feigning interest in the poker game while waiting for the man to raise his head so she could see his face clearly.

Finally, after staring at his cards for what seemed to her like hours, he looked at the player across the table from him and said, "I raise."

In her mind's eye she looked back on the original incident, when through a haze she had seen the faces of the men as they stood above her.

He was one of them!

When the hand was over and he had won the pot, he looked up at her and smiled. There was no hint of recognition in his eyes.

"See something you like, little lady?"

Gesturing with her beer mug, she said, "I'd like to get into this game — that is, I would if there was an empty seat available."

"That's no problem," the man said. He nudged the man seated to his immediate left, and the man quickly stood up and held the seat out for her. She could see his face clearly and identified him as another one of the six men.

"Thank you," she said, sitting down.

Where were the others? she wondered. Were they here in the saloon? Before she made any kind of move, she was going to have to determine that.

"Do you know the rules of the game, little lady?"

"I've played once or twice before."

"We're playing table stakes, three-raise limit."

"That's fine."

"I deal," he said, and proceeded to do so.

His face was not remarkable, just a plain, almost homely face, yet it had stuck in her mind as clear as could be over the past few weeks. Now she was here sitting next to him, with her property around his neck, and she couldn't do a thing about it.

Not yet, anyway.

As the game progressed she began to win, and the man began to smile less. When it wasn't her deal, she would scan the room with her eyes, and one by one she began to locate the other men.

There was one at the bar, talking to a saloon girl.

Two were seated at a table by the window.

And the sixth man had just gone upstairs with one of the girls.

She hoped that the man at the bar would eventually do the same thing, and it finally came to pass. As she watched him ascend the stair with his arm around the girl's waist, his hand clutching her right buttock, she felt that the time had come to move.

There were four of them present — one at the table with her, one standing behind him, watching, and the two by the window — but she had surprise on her side.

The funny thing was, she had not only won back all the money the man had taken from her, but more on top of it. Now she wanted that piece of metal around his neck, her father's Walker Colt . . . and revenge.

She had not seen the Walker Colt on either man at the poker table or on the men who had gone upstairs. It was conceivable that one of the men by the window had it, or else it was in someone's hotel room.

"You said you played this game once or twice before, missy," the man at the table said. "I get the feeling that you was understating the case."

"Not really," she said, shuffling the cards as she spoke. "Actually, I don't have to be very good to beat a tinhorn like you."

"Tinhorn!" the man said, narrowing his eyes and staring at her. Behind him the other man laughed.

"Tinhorn, thief, snake," she said, "take your pick, friend. They all fit you."

"You got no call to insult me, lady," the man said. "If you were a man I'd kill you for that."

"If I was a man I'd stand up and give you the beating you deserve."

"Now listen —" he said, but he was drowned out by the laughter at the table. He looked around him and noticed that they had attracted the attention of some of the patrons.

"Missy, if you wasn't a woman —"

"We went through that already, friend. I'm a woman and you're a poor excuse for a man. We've established that."

"Damn you. . . ." he said slowly.

"I'll tell you what," she said, still shuffling the cards. "Why don't we start by you giving me back what's mine, and maybe I won't have to kill you."

"What? What do I have that's yours?"

"That piece of metal around your neck," she said, and suddenly he froze.

"That's right," she said, "you and your five brave friends rode down one lone woman a few weeks back. Knocked her horse out from under her and robbed her. I'm surprised you didn't rape her while you were at it, but if you had you'd be dead already, because I would have killed you as soon as I saw you. As it stands now, you have a chance to walk out of here alive."

"That was you. . . ." he said.

She dropped a card from her shuffle and reached down to the floor to retrieve it.

"That was me," she said, nodding.

"Get her!" the man shouted, shoving his chair back from the table. In doing so he banged into his partner behind him, who had been in the act of drawing his gun. The back of the wooden chair struck the man on his gun hand, and he howled as his gun went spinning across the room.

Angel Eyes grabbed the leg of the table instead of the card on the floor and upended it. The other players all leapt back, wanting no part of what was going on now. The table struck the first man and knocked him off balance.

By the window, the other two men had seen what was happening and they were in the act of standing up, drawing their guns. As soon as they fired a shot, the two men upstairs would start to come down.

She had to act now.

Standing up, she drew her gun. The other patrons in the crowded saloon all hit the floor or scrambled out of the way, giving her a clear shot at the two by the window. She fired twice, striking them both in the chest. One man went back and, tripping over a chair, fell to the floor, dead. The other was driven back to where he hit the table, tumbled back over it, and then went through the window to the street outside.

The man who had been playing poker with her had recovered his balance and was frantically clawing for his gun. She shot him in the throat.

The fourth man was on his hands and knees trying to find his gun, and she shouted, "Don't try it!"

"Liz!" she heard someone shout behind her.

As she turned, she saw the two men on the steps, both of whom had their guns out. They had appeared sooner than she expected, probably because they'd been on their way down anyway. Now they were both preparing to fire at her, but before they could she heard gunfire from another direction.

Billy Quick had stood up from his table, drawn his gun, and fired at the two men. He struck one of the men in the shoulder, spinning him around and sending him tumbling down the steps. The second shot he fired was too hasty and went wild. The other man on the steps turned toward him to fire, but Bill kept his cool and fired again, his shot hitting the man in the chest. He tumbled down the steps and came to rest atop his friend.

The man on the floor had located his gun, and as he reached for it both Angel Eyes and Billy Quick converged on him, pointing their guns down at him.

"Don't try it," she said again, and the man rocked back on his heels and put his hands in the air.

"What the hell is going on here?" a man bellowed,

coming through the batwing doors. He wore a badge on his chest and, when he saw Liz and Billy, stalked over to them.

"Well?" he demanded.

"Just a friendly poker game, sheriff," Liz said. "With this man's help, I think I can explain exactly what happened — isn't that right?" she asked the man on the floor.

"Yes, ma'am," the man said. "Whatever you say."

"Then suppose you talk to the sheriff here, and start at the beginning."

CHAPTER THIRTY-SIX

"So you got all your belongings back?" Captain Barnaby asked her.

"And my money — and Billy here saved my life."

They were back in camp, regaling the entire company with the events at the saloon. The carnies were as spellbound as one of their own audiences.

"You should have seen Liz," Billy said. "She was incredible! Just like she was when she shot Purvis down."

Magda and Captain Barnaby and Liz all looked at Billy Quick in surprise. For the past two weeks he had not even spoken Purvis's name. Apparently he had felt it a mark of his shame that it had been Liz who had gunned Purvis down. For him to mention it now was a huge step in the right direction.

As had been his action back at the saloon.

"You did save my life, Billy," Liz said, "and I appreciate it. It was a very brave thing to do."

"I couldn't just let them kill you," Billy said with an embarrassed shrug.

Magda hugged him and beamed at Liz. She had her man back — oh, maybe not all the way back, but he was off to a hell of a start.

"What about the reward?" Edgar asked, changing the subject.

"We should have an answer later this evening or tomorrow, Edgar," Captain Barnaby said, "but right now we've got a show to get ready for."

"I wish luck to you all," Liz said.

Magda frowned.

"You sound as if you're leaving."

"I am. I was going to stay to watch your show tonight, but the sheriff sort of hinted that it would be best if I left town right away. I don't blame him, and I am sort of anxious to get moving again."

"Where will you go?" Billy asked as Captain Barnaby slipped away.

"I'll just travel, Billy," Liz said. "That's what I was doing when this whole mess started."

Magda released Billy and came forward to hug Liz, and then the others all came forward to say good-bye.

"I'll miss you all," she said, and turned to walk to where Blossom was waiting, all saddled and ready to go. Captain Barnaby was there, putting something into her saddlebag.

"A surprise gift?"

He turned quickly, embarrassed at having been caught.

"Just something I don't need anymore." He took his hand out of her saddlebag and showed her the pint bottle. "I figure you could use it better than me. You know how to handle the stuff." He smiled proudly then and said, "It's been a week since I had a drop."

She leaned in and kissed him, accepting the pint bottle.

"I'm proud of you, Captain, and I'm going to miss you. Good luck with your show."

As she mounted Blossom and looked down at him, he said, "I hope our paths cross again, Liz."

"That would be nice, wouldn't it?" she said, but as she wheeled Blossom around and rode out of camp, she doubted that it would ever happen.

GREAT BOOKS

E-BOOKS

AUDIOBOOKS

& MORE

Visit us today

www.speakingvolumes.us

www.ingramcontent.com/pod-product-compliance
Lightning Source LLC
Chambersburg PA
CBHW020611250626
47154CB00004B/1455